THE SINISTER PIG

ALSO BY TONY HILLERMAN

Fiction

The Wailing Wind
Hunting Badger
The First Eagle
The Fallen Man
Finding Moon
Sacred Clowns
Coyote Waits
Talking God
A Thief of Time
Skinwalkers
The Ghostway
The Dark Wind
People of Darkness
Listening Woman
Dance Hall of the Dead
The Fly on the Wall
The Blessing Way
The Boy Who Made Dragonfly (for children)

Nonfiction

Seldom Disappointed
Hillerman Country
The Great Taos Bank Robbery
Rio Grande
New Mexico
The Spell of New Mexico
Indian Country

THE SINISTER PIG

TONY HILLERMAN

HarperLargePrint
An Imprint of HarperCollins*Publishers*

THE SINISTER PIG. Copyright © 2003 by Tony Hillerman. All rights reserved. Printed in the United States of America. No part of this book may be used or reproduced in any manner whatsoever without written permission except in the case of brief quotations embodied in critical articles and reviews. For information, address HarperCollins Publishers Inc., 10 East 53rd Street, New York, NY 10022.

HarperCollins books may be purchased for educational, business, or sales promotional use. For information, please write: Special Markets Department, HarperCollins Publishers Inc., 10 East 53rd Street, New York, NY 10022.

FIRST HARPER LARGE PRINT EDITION

Printed on acid-free paper

Library of Congress Cataloging-in-Publication Data is available upon request.

ISBN 0-06-054543-7

03 04 05 06 07 DB/RD 10 9 8 7 6 5 4 3 2 1

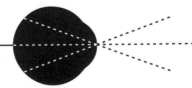

This Large Print Book carries the
Seal of Approval of N.A.V.H.

ACKNOWLEDGMENTS

A huge thanks goes to Maryanne Noonan, a veteran of the U.S. Customs Service, for her help relative to the efforts of our undermanned and overworked Border Patrol to stem the flood across our borders, and to Marty Nelson (my unpaid research specialist in Denver) for keeping me abreast of the Department of the Interior's efforts to explain what has happened to $176,000,000 (billions!!!) of Indian oil, gas, coal, timber, etc—royalties which it can't seem to acount for. Henry Schepers, an old friend and veteran pipeliner, also provided valuable aid on the laundering and trapping of pigs and other mysteries of that underground industry.

—Tony Hillerman

THE SINISTER PIG

1

David Slate reached across the tiny table in Bistro Bis and handed an envelope to the graying man with the stiff burr haircut.

"You are now Carl Mankin," Slate said. "You are newly retired from the Central Intelligence Agency. You are currently employed as a consultant for Seamless Weld. Along with your new credit card, Carl, that envelope holds a lot of authentic-looking stuff from Seamless. Business cards, expense account forms—that sort of material. But the credit card should cover any expenses."

"Carl Mankin," the burr-haired man said, inspecting the card. "And a Visa card. 'Carl Mankin' should be easy to remember. And by next Tuesday, I actually will be newly retired from the CIA." He was older than middle age, well past sixty, but trim, sunburned, and young looking. He sorted through the papers from the envelope and smiled at Slate. "However, I don't seem to find a contract in here," he said.

Slate laughed. "And I'll bet you didn't expect to find one, either. The senator works on the old-fashioned 'gentlemen's agreement' contract. You know, 'Your word's as good as your bond.' That sounds odd here in Washington these days, but some of the old-timers still like to pretend there is honor alive among the political thieves."

"Remind me of what that word is, then," the new Carl Mankin said. "As I remember it, you buy my time for thirty days, or until the job is done. Or failing that, I tell you it can't be done. And the pay is fifty thousand dollars, either way it works out."

"And expenses," Slate said. "But the credit card should cover that unless you're paying somebody to tell you something." He chuckled. "Somebody who doesn't accept a Visa card."

Carl Mankin put everything back into the envelope, and the envelope on the table beside his salad plate. "Who actually pays the credit card bill? I noticed my Carl Mankin address is in El Paso, Texas."

"That's the office of Seamless Weld," Slate said. "The outfit you're working for."

"The senator owns it? That doesn't sound likely."

"It isn't likely. It's one of the many sub-sidiaries of Searigs Corporation, and that, so I understand, is partly owned and totally con-trolled by A.G.H. Industries."

"Searigs? That's the outfit that built the off-shore-drilling platforms for Nigeria," said Carl Mankin. "Right?"

"And in the North Sea," Slate said. "For the Norwegians. Or was it the Swedish?"

"Owned by the senator?"

"Of course not. Searigs is part of A.G.H. Industries. What are you getting at, anyway?"

"I am trying to get at who I am actually working for."

Slate sipped his orange juice, grinned at Carl Mankin, said: "You surely don't think anyone would have told me that, do you?"

"I think you could guess. You're the senator's chief administrative aide, his picker of witnesses for the committees he runs, his doer of undigni-fied deeds, his maker of deals with the various lobbyists—" Mankin laughed. "And need I say it, his finder of other guys like me to run the senator's errands with somebody else paying the fee. So I surely do think you could make an accurate guess. But would you tell me if you did?"

Slate smiled. "Probably not. And I am almost certain you wouldn't believe me if I told you."

"In which case, I should probably make sure to get my pay in advance."

Slate nodded. "Exactly. When we finish lunch, and you pay for it with your new Visa card, we'll go down to the bank I use. We transfer forty-nine thousand five hundred dollars into Carl Mankin's account there, and I present you the deposit slip."

"And the other five hundred?"

Slate got out his wallet, extracted a deposit slip, and handed it to Carl Mankin. It showed a Carl Mankin account opened the previous day with a five-hundred-dollar deposit. Mankin put it in his shirt pocket, then took it out and laid it on the table.

"An account opened for an imaginary man without his signature. I didn't know that could be done."

Slate laughed. "It's easy if the proper vice president calls down from upstairs and says do it."

"We need to be clear about this," Mankin

said. "You want me to go out to that big Four Corners oil patch in New Mexico, look it over, see if I can find out how the pipeline system out there was used—and maybe still is being used— to bypass paying royalty money into the Interior Department's trust fund for the Indians. Does that about summarize the job?"

Slate nodded.

"That's a big part of it. The most important information of all is the names of those switching the stuff around so the money for it goes into the right pockets. And who owns the pockets."

"And the senator understands that this is likely to produce nothing. I presume it is one of a whole bunch of ways he's looking for some way to pin the blame, or the corruption, on somebody for that four- or five-billion-dollar loss of royalty money from the Tribal Trust Funds. The one the **Washington Post** has been writing about for the past month. The one the Secretary of Interior and the Bureau of Indian Affairs honchos are in trouble over."

Slate was grinning again. "Was that intended as a question? What do the press secretaries say to questions like that?" He slipped into a serious, disapproving expression. "We never comment on speculation."

"The newspapers say that this ripping off the four billion or so of Tribal royalty money has been going on for more than fifty years. And they're quoting the government bean counters. Right? I can't see much hope of me finding anything new."

"It's not a mere four billion dollars," Slate said. "The Government Accounting Office estimated the amount not accounted for may be as high as forty billion. And the law firm for the tribes is now claiming the U.S. gov has stacked up a debt of a hundred and thirty-seven billion bucks on royalties dating back to 1887. I guess what the senator wants to know is if the stealing persists."

"And he bets somebody's fifty grand that I'll be lucky enough to find out."

"His friends in the State Department tell him you did a great job finding out how Iraqi oil people switched pipelines to avoid those United Nations' sanctions on exporting their oil. I guess he just wants you to do it again."

"It's a very different story out there," Carl Mankin said. "In the Middle East oil patch you had a small bunch of greasy old pipeline experts surrounded by various groups of Arabs. The Arabs weren't really members of the Brit-

American petroleum club. Which I was. Everybody knew everybody's business. After twenty years in and out of there, I was just another one of them. People talked to me. I got sneaked into pipeline switching stations, got to see pressure gauges—all the technical stuff. Out in New Mexico, I'll just be a damned nosey stranger."

Slate was studying him. He grinned. "In New Mexico, you'll be Carl Mankin. Right? All this making apologies in advance for not finding anything useful means you're signing on?"

"Oh, sure. I guess so," he said. He folded the deposit slip into his wallet, took out the Carl Mankin Visa card, signaled to the waiter, and then handed the card to him when the waiter came to the table.

"A symbolic action," Slate said, and laughed.

"One more thought I want to pass along," he said. "What little chance I have out there of picking up any useful information would be multiplied many times over if I had a clearer idea, a more specific idea, of what he wants."

"Just the truth," Slate said. "Nothing but the truth."

"Yeah," Carl Mankin said. "But I'm entertaining all kinds of thoughts. For example, why connect me directly with this Texas construction outfit? Seamless Weld. Sounds like something in the pipelining business. Does the senator own it?"

"I'm sure he wouldn't," said Slate. "It will be owned by some corporation that is part of a conglomerate in which the senator has a substantial interest. If he actually owned Seamless Weld on any public record, he'd be way too sly to get it involved."

They were on the sidewalk now, hailing a cab, a warm breeze moving dust along the street, the smell of rain in the air.

"So why stick me with that company? And don't tell me it's to make my expenses tax deductible. What's the reason?"

A cab stopped for them. Slate opened the door, ushered Mankin in, seated himself, gave the driver the bank's address, settled back, and said: "Looks like rain."

"I'm waiting for an answer," Mankin said. "And it's not just out of curiosity. "I'm going to be asking a lot of questions, and that means I'll have to answer a lot of them myself. I can't afford to be caught lying."

"OK," Slate said. He took a little silver cigarette box out of his coat pocket, opened it, offered one to Mankin, took one himself, looked at it, put it back in the box, and said: "Well, I guess you know that everyone in this town has at least two agendas. The public one, and their own personal causes. Right?"

Mankin nodded.

"OK, then. Let's say you called your broker and asked him who owned Seamless Weld. He'd call you back in a few days and tell you it was a subsidiary of Searigs Inc. And you'd say, who owns Searigs, and after the proper period for checking, he'd tell you the principal stockholder was A.G.H. Industries Inc. And the answer to your next question is that the majority stock holder in A.G.H. is a trust, the affairs of which are entrusted to a Washington law firm, and the law firm lists four partners, one of whom is Mr. Rawley Winsor of Washington, D.C. End of answer."

"I've heard that name. But who is Rawley Winsor?"

"No genuine Washington insider would have to ask that," Slate said. "Nor would anyone on Wall Street. Rawley Winsor is . . . How do I start? He's a many-generations blue blood, echelons of high society, Princeton, then Harvard Law, famous Capitol deal doer, fund-raisers, top-level runner of lobby campaigns, and might make the top of **Fortune** magazine's most-wealthy list if his investments weren't so carefully hidden."

"So if I was free to speculate, I might guess that your senator is either doing a deal for this Winsor plutocrat, or seeking a way to link him with evildoing. For example, maybe finding how to prove this guy is getting a slice of the suspected rip-off of tribal royalty funds. Or maybe a way for the senator to get his own cut of that graft."

Slate laughed. "I am not free to comment on speculation."

"But if he is so incredibly rich, why go to all this trouble for what must be just small change for him?"

"Joy of the game, maybe," Slate said. "Hell, I don't know. Maybe Winsor just can't stand seeing some other power broker getting easy money that he's not sharing. Right now, for example, everybody knows he's running the lobby against a bill to legalize medical use of marijuana. Why? Because he's afraid it would lead to legalizing drugs—making them government licensed, taxed, et cetera. Why is he against that? Lot of people are, because it has proven to be a counterproductive waste of public money. But that wouldn't be Winsor's motive. Nobody knows what that is. Not for sure. But we Washington cynics think it's because he has a finger in the narcotics import trade. Legalizing and licensing knocks out the profits. Government sells it at fixed prices, grows it in the farm belt, taxes the hell out of it. No more recruiting of new addicts by your teenaged salesmen, no more knife fights and gun battles for market territory." Slate sighed. "Not that any of that matters."

"Come on, now," Mankin said. "This guy is a multibillionaire. Dabbling in the drug trade isn't just a fun competition. I can't believe he'd be that dumb."

"Probably not," Slate said. "Maybe it's psychological. My wife has three pet cats. One of them will eat all he can hold, and then stand guard at the bowl to keep the other two from having their dinner. Snarl, and claw to fight 'em off. Are humans smarter than cats?"

Mankin nodded. "You know any farmyard French?"

"Just English for me," Slate said.

"Anyway, French farmers have a phrase for the boss pig in the sty—the one that would guard the trough and attack any animal that tried to steal a bite. Translate it to French and it's **porc sinistre.** We used to use that for Saddam—for trying to take Iran's oil fields when he had more oil than he could use, and then invading Kuwait for the same reason."

" 'Sinister pig,' right?" Slate asked. "But isn't it **cochon sinistre.** I think that makes a better insult. And it would fit Rawley Winsor, from what I hear about him."

That lunch and conversation had been on Monday. The newly named Carl Mankin called his wife to tell her he'd be going to New Mexico for several days. Then he took a taxi to the Department of Energy, called on the proper friend, and collected the information he needed about who managed which pipelines and the ebb and flow, sales and resales, of oil and gas in and out of the San Juan Basin fields. He left the building with his pocket recorder full of notes about the San Juan Basin fields—about nineteen hundred oil, gas, and methane wells actively producing in just the New Mexico section of that field, and drilling rigs adding new ones every year, with geologists estimating that more than a hundred trillion cubic feet of gas is under the rocks there, and about twenty different oil, gas, and pipeline companies fighting for a share of the treasure. Making the job look even more impossible, his notes confirmed what he'd guessed would be true. The records kept by the Department of the Interior were in shambles, and had been a total mess dating back as far as his sources had looked—which was into the 1940s. It was hopeless, he thought, but for fifty thousand dollars whether he learned anything or not, it would be an interesting project.

And now it was two Mondays later. He was about fifteen hundred miles west of the chic Bistro Bis of the Hotel George and Washington's E Street. He was sitting in a Jeep Cherokee beside a dirt road at the fringe of the Bisti Oil-Gas field, close to where the Jicarilla Apache reservation meets the Navajo Nation in the very heart of America's version of the Persian Gulf—the San Juan Basin.

More important, Carl Mankin had just realized he was being followed—and that this had been going on since the evening after he'd left the Seamless Weld office in El Paso in the rental Jeep. It was a bad feeling for Carl Mankin. He'd learned how to spot a tail more than thirty years ago in Lebanon, taught by an old CIA hand in the Beirut embassy. He'd practiced the skill of

being invisible in Iraq when Saddam and his
Republican Guards were fighting the Iranians as
our Cold War ally. He'd used it again when
Saddam was becoming our Desert Storm enemy, and refined it to perfection in Yemen,
where the Al Qaeda was plotting its terrorism.
He had become very good at knowing who was
walking behind him.

But two lazy years in Washington must have
made him careless. Across the street from the
Seamless Weld office he'd seen the man now
tailing him, noticing him because he wore a
forked beard and not because Mankin suspected
anything. He saw him again when he came out
of the FBI office in Gallup—in a car in the parking lot. He'd seen that forked beard a third time
a few minutes ago, the face of a man sitting on
the passenger side of a Dodge pickup reflected
in the rearview mirror of the Jeep Cherokee
Mankin was driving.

Three sightings at three very different loca-
tions were too many for coincidence. Of course,
the man had to be a rank amateur. No professional would wear such a memorable beard.
Probably no danger involved here. Why would
there be danger? It would just be someone wanting to know why a stranger was looking into a

very lucrative and competitive business. But those old instincts of caution Mankin developed working in enemy territory had abruptly revived. The man had gotten on his trail at Seamless Weld in El Paso. How? Or why?

One isn't followed for love and kindness. Perhaps the senator, or whomever the senator was working for, connected him to Seamless because they suspected that company was involved in the corruption. Thus that would be the place to start him looking for connections.

He watched the pickup roll past on the road just below him, Forked Beard out of his line of vision. Its driver, a younger man wearing a blue baseball cap, glanced at the Cherokee and quickly looked away. Just the sort of thing professionals were taught never to do.

Carl Mankin waited, listening to the pickup moving slowly down the dirt road, hearing the crows quarreling in the pines and the sounds of the breeze in the trees. Relaxing. Feeling the old familiar tension slip away. He stepped out of the Jeep, listening. The crows left. The breeze faded. Mankin held his breath. Silence. How could the truck have gotten out of hearing range so quickly? Perhaps in a thicker patch of forest. Perhaps down a slope.

Some of the tension had returned now, but Mankin had driven two hours to reach this place. The metal structure across the road from him, so he'd been told by the driver of a Haliburton repair truck, was a pipeline junction switching point. "A lot of work going on out there," the man had said. "Installing some new measurement stuff and a bigger compressor. Why the hell would they be doing that? I couldn't guess."

Mankin couldn't guess either. But the "new measurement stuff" suggested a possibility that maybe the old measurements had been less than accurate, and maybe that had been intentional, to cover up some cheating on the records, and maybe that was the sort of thing he was looking for. Probably not. But he'd come this far. He would walk over and see what he could see.

He stopped that short walk twice to listen. He heard the sound the breeze made in the pines and crows arguing a long way down the road. Otherwise nothing. The building was locked, as he'd guessed it would be, since no vehicles were parked there. He peered through the dusty window and saw what he'd expected to see. A compressor, tanks, gauges, a worktable, pipes of various dimensions, valves, etcetera.

Just what he had seen in such places in oil-patch country from the Middle East to Alaska to Indonesia to Wyoming. But he saw no sign of any work currently going on.

He was recrossing the road, almost back to the Jeep, when he saw Forked Beard for the fourth time. The man was standing under the trees beyond the Jeep, the younger man in the blue baseball cap stood beside him. Both men were looking at him. Blue Cap held a rifle and the rifle was swinging toward him.

Carl Mankin spun into a running crouch. Old as he was, he was quick. He made at least a dozen long running steps before the bullet hit him, midback, between the shoulder blades, and knocked him facedown into the dirt.

2

"Well, look at this," said Cowboy Dashee, grinning up at Sergeant Jim Chee. "I'll bet that any minute now you're going to be asking me to go ahead and handle this guy. Doing me a favor. Giving me a chance to keep my hand in on such things as murder."

Dashee was standing beside the body of a medium-sized male, gray-blond hair cut into a burr, sprawled facedown in a brushy growth of mountain mahogany, partly covered with dead leaves and debris, maybe by the wind or maybe for concealment.

"Feel free," said Chee. "You probably could use a refresher on your crime scene technique now that you're sort of a bureaucrat."

Dashee was a Hopi, and thus untroubled by Chee's traditional Navajo aversion to handling corpses, and Dashee might have been wearing the uniform of his Federal Bureau of Land Management law-enforcement unit. Today he was off duty and in his more casual attire—jeans and well-worn T-shirt. He'd been drinking coffee in Chee's Navajo Tribal Police Shiprock office when Chee's telephone buzzed. An El Paso Natural Gas employee had noticed a dead man in a ditch out northeast of Degladito Mesa where Navajo country bumps into the Jicarilla Apache Reservation.

"Notice how careful I am with your crime scene," Dashee said. "I avoid stepping where whoever hauled our victim in here stepped. Or where the victim himself might have stepped when he walked in here to kill himself."

"OK," Chee said. "Get on with it."

"I'm not always so careful," Dashee said, "but this is probably a felony murder on the Navajo Reservation, which means the FBI is going to take over soon as somebody tells them about it, and if it turns out to be a tough case, then the Bureau will need someone to blame when they screw it up. I don't want it to be Officer Cowboy Dashee. Been there and done that back when I was a deputy sheriff."

"So far you've been flawless," Chee said, watching Dashee checking the body.

"Hole in the back of jacket," Dashee said. "Probably the entry place. But no blood that I can see and no powder marks. I'll get some close-up photos before I move the body."

"I'll go call it in," Chee said.

"I'm avoiding my usual sloppiness because I'm remembering all the trouble your girlfriend got into. Officer Bernie thinking the guy in the truck was just another dead drunk, instead of a shot-dead drunk." Dashee paused to chuckle at his pun. "And the shot wasn't from a whiskey glass."

"I guess you're talking about Officer Manuelito," Chee said, no longer looking amused. "She's not my girlfriend."

"I heard she'd left you. I meant girlfriend then. Meant 'used-to-be' girlfriend."

"Not then, either," Chee said. "She worked for me. You don't make moves on women who work for you."

"You don't?" said Dashee, making it sound surprised. But Chee was already walking back to his car radio.

He gave the FBI dispatcher directions to the scene.

"Highway 64 east through Gobernador, then through Vaqueros Canyon nine miles, then left over a cattle guard on dirt gas field road. Seven miles north to junction with another dirt road that leads to El Paso Gas Buzzard Wash lease. Left on that. He'll see my unit parked there."

"It'll be Special Agent Osborne," the dispatcher said. "I'll tell him to call you when he gets lost."

Dashee had walked down the slope from the crime scene, dusting off his hands and grinning.

"How much do you usually pay the shaman when he does the Ghost Way sing for you to cure you of corpse sickness?" Dashee asked. "I think that might be an appropriate tip to give me."

"I'll just deduct that from what I was going to charge you for the crime scene lesson," Chee said.

"Well, you've got yourself a whole lot of work before you're finished with this fellow here. No identification. No wallet. Expensive duds. Pockets empty except car keys."

Chee raised his eyebrows. "Car keys but no car?"

"Lots of legwork ahead," Dashee said, "and without pretty little Bernie Manuelito for you to send out here to do it for you. Maybe you could borrow her back from the Border Patrol."

3

The week Bernadette Manuelito quit being a Navajo Tribal Police Officer and became a Customs Patrol Officer, her new supervisor had suggested that Rodeo, a village just on the New Mexico side of the Arizona border, would be a fine place for her to live. It would be handy to the section of U.S.–Mexico border she would be patrolling and Customs Officer Eleanda Garza already lived there. Mrs. Garza's two-bedroom house had one bedroom empty and was available due to the resignation of Customs Officer Dezzie Something-or-Other—Dezzie having quit to marry some fellow in Tucson.

Mrs. Garza was a member of Tohono O'odham Nation, which had been called the Papagos ("The Bean Eaters"), a name given the tribe by the Spanish in the sixteenth century.

They had voted in 1980 to resume their traditional name (in English, "The Desert People") and the sentiment for that was overwhelming. Mrs. Garza was older than Bernadette, larger by about twenty pounds, and married to a telephone company maintenance man—her second husband—who lived and worked at Las Cruces. Her son was a new recruit in navy boot camp in San Diego, and her daughter was far away in Chicago, where her son-in-law worked for the **Chicago Tribune** circulation department. This had left Eleanda Garza suffering the "empty nest syndrome."

Thus, even though the Desert People are reputed to be sort of hostile to Navajos and Apaches (and vice versa) by the end of the first week as housemates, Mrs. Garza had developed a liking for Bernie.

The feeling was mutual. Bernie was homesick. Her own traditional name was "Girl Who Laughs," but lately she rarely did. She missed her mother, people she worked with at the Shiprock office of the Navajo Tribal Police, and her girlfriends. Although she hated to admit it, she also missed Sergeant Jim Chee.

Mrs. Garza had spotted that the very first day they talked, when Bernie explained why she had changed jobs. Bernie had described the last case she had been involved in—her very first homicide—how she had bungled the crime scene, and how she had been shot at herself, or thought she had been, anyway. She also described the dreadful shock of finding—locked in one of those miles of mostly empty army ammunition bunkers at old Fort Wingate—the mummified body of a young wife who had written love notes to her husband while she starved to death in the silent darkness.

"I just couldn't stand any more of that," Bernie had said. Mrs. Garza had sensed, instantly, that there was more to it than the tragedy involved in the case. But she was too kind (or wise) to press. Not then, anyway. It wasn't until Eleanda was driving Bernie along the track that runs along the U.S. side of Mexican border fence that the truth emerged.

They had been bumping along the absolute southernmost bottom of New Mexico's so-called boot heel. For hours Bernie had been mostly silent. She'd seen no evidence of human existence except the steel fence posts and three (sometimes two) strands of the barbed wire stretched between them. Dry, ragged mountains to the south in Sonora, northward in New

Mexico, the same ahead, same behind. Bernie had a weakness for botany, her major study at the University of New Mexico, and this landscape was interesting as well as hostile. Various varieties of cacti, with little herds of javlina browsing on the pods of some of them, clumps of gray and tan desert grasses waving their autumn seed stems, the orderly scattering of creosote bush, and species of mesquite new to her and swarming with bees attracted by the honey in the flowers, and brush with more thorns than leaves. Bernie was accustomed to empty country, but Dinetah, her "Land Between the Sacred Mountains," was greener, friendlier, had at least a few people in it. Philosophers teach that lonely country wears on friendly people.

Eleanda was sympathetic. She had been stopping now and then to show trails illegals used, pointing to examples of the deeper heel prints, the shorter paces and the wider stances that suggested "mules" carrying heavy loads of cocaine or heroin had mixed with the immigrants to use them as cover. She knelt where the limbs of a thorny bush intruded into the trail—showed Bernie a thorn that held a tiny clump of fiber.

"That's an acacia," Bernie said. "The catclaw acacia. I forget the scientific name. But the one people try to grow is the desert acacia. Has beautiful yellow flowers. Very fragrant."

Eleanda laughed. "And right there, that vine to your left with those beautiful white blossoms, that's sacred datura. You know. The psychedelic. The little button seeds, if you chew them, or brew them, they send you off into visions."

"As in the rites of the Native American Church," Bernie said. "I tried that when I was in college." She shuddered. "How can a flower that beautiful produce something that tastes so terrible?"

"Datura used to be on the illegal substances list," Eleanda said. "Until the court ruled it was a religious sacrament. But forget the datura. I was showing you the cloth," she said.

"Cloth?"

"These fibers caught on the claw are from a gunny sack. The drug smugglers use potato sacks to carry the dope in."

Bernie nodded.

"The illegals, they're good people. They just can't get work in Mexico and their families are hungry. They don't have guns. Wouldn't hurt anybody if they did. But when you see this"— she pulled the fiber from a thorn—"then you're not just tracking illegal immigrants going north to look for a job. Then you should be very careful."

"I'm careful," Bernie said, and produced a wry smile. "That's exactly what Sergeant Chee told me when I left. 'Be very careful.' That's all he said."

"That's the sergeant you told me about? Did you talk to him about coming down here?"

"I didn't talk to him about it."

"You didn't? What you told me made him sound very nice. But I guess you don't like him? He was bad to you, wasn't he?"

"No. No. No," Bernie said. "It wasn't that. Really, he's very kind. Very . . ." She paused. How could she express this?

"Kind? To you?"

"I didn't mean that. He was my boss."

"So kind to who?"

Bernie shrugged. "Well, pretty much everybody."

"Like how, for example."

"Well, I didn't see this myself," Bernie said. "But it's a story people tell about him. He had a hit-and-run homicide case. Real strange one. There's a radio station at Farmington that has an open mike program. People who want to invite people to a curing ceremony, or buy a horse, or sell baled hay, they just go in and the station lets them use the mike. So this fugitive driver does that. He goes in and broadcasts that he is the man who ran over the fellow beside the road and drove off and left the body. He said he was too drunk to know what he was doing, and he is sorry, and that every month he will send part of his paycheck to the man's family."

"Really!" Eleanda said. "I wish we had that kind of drunks. But did he actually send money?"

"Two hundred dollars every month," Bernie said. "But Sergeant Chee still had this homicide case to solve. Nobody at the open mike station had recognized him, but they remembered he smelled like onions. Jim went to Navajo Agricultural Project onion warehouse and described the bumper stickers on the truck, and the people there told him who owned it. Jim went to his place. He wasn't home but his grandson was there. An emotionally disturbed boy named Don the grandfather was raising. So Jim had another set of bumper stickers printed. Stuff like 'Don Is My Hero.' You know? And he gave 'em to the boy and told him to have his granddad change the stickers because the police would arrest him if he kept using the old ones."

Story finished, Bernie looked at Eleanda, gauging her reaction. And Eleanda looked at Bernie. She saw large and beautiful brown eyes, a little sad now, the perfect oval face popular for cosmetics commercials, and a shape that looked fine even in the Border Patrol uniform. A sweet girl. This Sergeant Chee must be blind or retarded. She shook her head.

"Pretty risky for a cop to do that," Eleanda said. "You think it actually happened like that?"

"Yes," Bernie said. "It's just like him."

"Doing something like that could cost you your job. Worse than that, you're destroying evidence in a felony case. You're risking—"

"I know," Bernie said. "I didn't say he was smart. I just said he was kind." And then, being tired, confused, homesick, lonely, and unhappy, she started to cry, and Eleanda hugged her.

"Men are so damned stupid," Eleanda said.

A minute or two later, after finding a handkerchief and wiping her eyes, Bernie looked up and nodded.

"Most of them, I guess. But not all. My mother's father, Hostiin Yellow. I guess you'd call him my godfather. The one in Navajo culture who gives us our real name, the name we use in ceremonies. We get that name when we're old enough to smile, and it's a secret. After that awful business at the bunker, Hostiin Yellow had a curing ceremony for me. A Ghost Way, we call it, and it cured me. So I could sleep without dreams and feel normal again. I think I should go and talk to him."

Mrs. Garza hugged her again, and smiled at her. "Ask Hostiin Yellow if he can cure you of being lonesome for your man."

4

Rawley Winsor had put the e-mail printout on his desk and was staring across it through his office window, focused on the distant dome of the Capitol. The e-mail concerned one of the issues on his list of today's chores. It had added to an unpleasant feeling that things were slipping out of control. Winsor hated not being in control.

Even the schedule for today was already off-beat. On his notepad he listed an agenda of problems to be dealt with:

1. War on Drugs. Haret?
2. Chrissy. Budge.
3. Reassure Bank. call V.P. for M.C.
4. Four Corners. Mex lawyer.

Come to think of it, the e-mail concerned all the same problem. Everything but Chrissy. And now Chrissy had been handled properly and neatly, with no residual loose ends left to complicate matters. He drew a line through "Chrissy. Budge." and renumbered items 3 and 4, making them 2 and 3. He could draw a line through CHRISSY because in that one he had kept control himself. He had assigned it to a man who was solidly, and stolidly, under control. A valuable keeper, Budge. But the other three problems had all grown out of assigning jobs to people he had no handle on.

He had assigned a really important project to people he was never sure he could trust—either for honesty or competence—because he didn't have a hammer held over their heads. As a result 3,644 pounds 11 ounces of his cocaine, neatly packaged in one-liter Baggies, had been loaded on a rusty trawler at Puerto Cortez in Belize, and the trawler had blown its old diesel engine. He had the trawler towed into a wharf at Vera Cruz, sent one of his A.G.H. Industries lawyers flying down there to arrange a secure way to get the coke into the A.G.H. warehouse outside Mexico City. All that represented more than $400,000 in needless costs, and at least a hundred hours of his own time. The cost of developing a secure way to get that coke out of Mexico, where it was worth maybe $5,000 a liter, into the U.S. market, where it was selling for $28,000 a liter as of yesterday in Washington, was even more expensive. That ran into the millions, and it wasn't over yet.

Winsor made a deprecatory clicking sound. The retail price in the District of Columbia had dropped $2,000 a liter in just two months, the slide starting as soon as that move to legalize medical marijuana began looking serious. If the bill passed, the fear of genuine federal control of all narcotics would spread, sending the wholesaler's price to the bottom. There was too much big money against it to keep even that mild little marijuana bill from passing now, he was pretty sure of that, but even the fear of it was already costing him. He did the math in his head: 3,644 pounds, at 2.206 pounds per kilo, made 1,656 kilograms. The $20,000 per kilo he could now count on in bulk price to wholesalers would bring in $33 million if the value held. He had less than $9 million invested so far. Even if he wrote off the trawler as a total loss—which it probably would be—the deal would be a big winner. And most of the remaining expenses were in a capital property, repeatedly useful if he stayed in the importing business. If he didn't, he could rent it to other importers.

He leaned back, away from that, and thought about Budge. It was unfortunate he hadn't known him well enough when this all started to understand what a good hand he was. He'd taken him in partly because he could fly the company plane as well as drive, and mostly because he had a handle on the man, and Budge knew it. Budge could have taken the company's yacht down to Belize, loaded the coke onto it, and sailed right up the Florida coast to the A.G.H. dock south of Jacksonville.

A thoughtful man, Budge. Perfectly efficient. No residual messiness left behind to nag you. Clean cut. Done with. Just as the Chrissy problem was done. Thinking of that cheered him up.

Budge had rolled Winsor's limo into the driveway of the town house this morning exactly on schedule, and stood there, holding the door open and smiling so calmly Winsor had wondered for a moment if he'd actually done the job.

Physically, Budge was the sort of man Winsor had dreamed in his boyhood he could become: six foot plus, quick, graceful, agile, with a handsome, tan, intelligent face.

Winsor had said: "Well? How about Chrissy? Did it go well?"

Budge had laughed and said: "Boss, I'm hurt that you even asked me such a question. Chrissy bothers you no more."

Problem solved.

The War on Drugs problem wasn't so easy. It had to be won over and over again as long as he stayed in the importing business. The sensitive subcommittee session dealing with that war was opening just about now. Haret should be there representing Winsor's interests. Winsor's interest was in keeping the War on Drugs alive, well funded, and managed with the same bungling incompetence that had filled the prison system with bottom-level dealers and users, and left the big operators untroubled and the price of cocaine and heroin profitably high. Not much in pot. Nickels and dimes. But it was on the list of "controlled substances" and had to be protected.

His grandfather had fattened the family fortune handling whiskey shipments during prohibition. Repeal destroyed that industry, put booze in licensed liquor stores, taxed it to death, and took out the profit. If the country actually "controlled" pot, the next step would be to actually control cocaine and heroin where the money was. That would happen some day. Winsor had decided that once he got this shipment safely into the country he'd consider dropping out of the trade.

Haret understood all that. But would Haret be working at the committee meeting? Would he be alert? Winsor had seen Haret at the French Embassy party last night heavily into the champagne. Worse he'd seen Haret on the moonlit balcony outside the ballroom passing a snort of cocaine to the pretty little senatorial assistant he had brought with him. Poor place for that. Poor judgment. Winsor had known Haret since their days at Harvard Law, but he'd have to find another lobbyist. Too bad Haret wasn't another Budge.

Winsor sighed. Back to problem 4, now numbered 3. He reread the printout. "Your 'cause for alarm' is now dealt with." Only that. Winsor remembered the argument and his anger at the obtuseness of his man in Juarez.

"I don't want to hear any more 'maybe this' and 'maybe it's only,'" Winsor had told the

Mexican. "Having someone snooping around makes me uneasy. It is cause for alarm. Deal with it." The Mexican's answer had been a moment of telephone silence, then a chuckle, and his man had said: "This nosey fellow is causing you alarm? OK. Shame on him. We will deal with it. Mark him off."

Winsor hadn't liked the sound of that nor the sarcasm. He liked this terse e-mail note even less. He thought about responding with an e-mail question. Perhaps "How?" or "Explain." But the Mexican might be stupid enough to be overly precise and he didn't want that "how," if it was what he suspected, to ·be in print anywhere.

Then he thought again of the erasure of his Chrissy problem. That restored some of his good spirits.

In the limo, he had slid the panel open and asked Budge for the details. Budge had chuckled.

"Boss, are you getting careless? I'm always speechless in this car." With that he handed a folded sheet of paper back over his shoulder through the panel.

Budge's attitude about not talking business in the limo was an argument Budge had won.

It had gone like this:

Winsor: "Why not. You keep it locked and garaged. Nobody could get to it to get a tap into it."

Budge, smiling at him: "Except you, Boss."

Winsor, frowning: "What the hell you mean by that?"

Budge, still smiling: "Think of me at a grand jury. I'm under oath. I am facing a possible perjury indictment. The prosecutor asks me—"

Winsor: "OK, I see what you mean."

Now Winsor opened the folded note.

Arrived at 9 A.M. Subject was ready with small suitcase and purse, smiling, giggling. Insisted on chattering.

At airport, put subject in back of plane. Used chloroform while buckling subject in. Went on autopilot off coast at 8 thousand. Used a bit more chloro. Removed subject's duds. Added that to the stuff in her suitcase. Put in two lead ingots. One ingot in purse. Flew deep water. Ejected suitcase and purse. Flew to ten miles, assured no air or watercraft in sight. Ejected subject. Windexed all points in aircraft possibly touched. Landed. Went home.

Ejected subject.

Winsor flinched at that. Glanced up at the back of Budge's head. Had the man looked back to see Chrissy's body falling? In his own imagination Winsor saw it tumbling toward the water, saw the splash. He shook his head, erasing the image. This wasn't like him, this sudden sentiment. But Chrissy had been with him more than a year. They'd had great times together at his place in Florida while his wife was doing her annual London-Paris-Milan fashion-shopping binge. But Budge had known her only from the times he'd been sent to pick her up or drive her home. No reason for sentiment. Quite different situation for Budge.

Winsor had moved across the seat to a position from which he could see Budge's face in the mirror. His expression was relaxed, unreadable.

Winsor leaned to the intercom. "Did you look back? Watch her fall?"

"What?" Budge sounded surprised. "Why? Something falls out of an airplane, there's no place to go but down." Then Budge shook his head. He had been smiling.

Winsor considered that.

Winsor compared it with his own reaction. Well, he hadn't had the sort of experience

Budge would have gone through flying for the Guatemala military, or whoever he was flying for, in that endless war against that country's crop of rural rebels. Budge had never talked about that—at least not to him—but it must have been pretty heavy stuff to get him a place on the Human Rights investigators' list of government war criminals. Unless the CIA arranged that when they needed to get rid of him. Something to keep their handle on him. No doubt lots of indiscriminate killings went on in those rainy mountains. Anyway, it had all worked out well for him. The CIA had gotten Budge out of Guatemala, into Washington, and onto the payroll of one of a war hawk congressman's committees as a temporary. And Winsor had made a powerful friend by hiring him as a favor to the congressman.

It had proved to be a favor to himself. A man he could count on to get a job done right. And a man who could be trusted, too—as far as Winsor could trust anyone. And Winsor could trust Budge because he came with a gun at his head and Winsor's finger on the trigger. All Winsor had to do to draw the line through Budge, just as he had drawn it through Chrissy, was call a certain man in the Secretary of State's office, who'd call the Guatemalan Embassy, and Budge would be flying south in handcuffs to a Guatemala jail. Of course Budge knew this. Thus Budge was trustworthy.

Budge, smiling still, was tearing the note in fragments, which he put into his mouth, chewed, and swallowed. Endlessly careful, Winsor thought. Burly as Budge was, even with Chrissy being a little thing, she might have been hard to handle in the close quarters of his Falcon 10. Bringing along the chloroform to put her to sleep was smart. Why take risks in a little plane. A dependable workman, Budge. Then he had another thought and spoke into the intercom.

"You told me you had five of those lead weights. You mentioned three."

He heard Budge sigh. Then he stuck up his hand, snapped his fingers, said: "Gimme some paper."

Winsor clipped the notebook page to the clasp on his fountain pen, handed it back through the window. Budge scribbled and handed it over his shoulder.

The scrawl read: "Wired to cuffs on wrists."

Winsor relaxed into the comfort of the limo seat. Pretty girl, Chrissy. Fun. Had she really gotten pregnant? Maybe. Anyway she was strongly into marrying him. Determined. Making lightly veiled threats. He had imagined her running, tears falling, to tell his wife. Not that Margo would have given a damn. But it would have given her a huge advantage if she wanted to divorce him. And Margo represented old money, and big money, and good connections. Even better than his own.

He'd miss Chrissy. But Vassar, and Bennington, and Smith, and Holyoke, and the rest of them turned a new crop out every spring. Smart, stylish, good families—everything. But he'd wait a bit before he'd adopt another one. That problem was solved. He'd concentrate on solving the others before hunting himself another congressional intern.

5

Captain Largo's instructions on the subject of cooperation with the FBI were clear and emphatic. "When you have to work with a Fed, use his car, not ours."

That explained why Sergeant Jim Chee was sitting in the passenger side of a dark blue Ford sedan, with Special Agent Oz Osborne of the Federal Bureau of Investigation behind the wheel. The automobile, a type favored by the Bureau since as far back as memory went, had been parked all morning amid an infinity of sage brush on the slope above the Huerfano Trading Post. It was a pleasant location with a fine view of the business establishment below, of traffic speeding along New Mexico Highway 44, of Chaco Mesa far to the west, and the sacred Turquoise Mountain rising against the sky beyond that. North. Visible through the side window were the towering walls of Huerfano Mesa.

The view was why they were there, with the focus being on the trading post and the highway. Their orders were more detailed than Largo's had been.

If an old pale blue Volkswagen camper van showed up below them—either emerging from Navajo Route 7500, which wandered through the Bisti Oil Field, or on U.S. 44, they would drive down to the highway, stop the van, and check the credit cards of everyone in it. If anyone had Visa card number 0087-4412-8703, made out to Carl Mankin, this person would be held. Osborne's superior in Gallup would be immediately notified. The van occupants would be taken to Farmington and held for questioning. If no one had this credit card, all would be taken into the Huerfano Trading Post, and the employees there would be asked if any of them resembled the fellow who had stopped at the post in the blue van on two recent occasions buying gasoline with the Mankin card in the "pay at pump" computer, which didn't ask for card-owner signatures.

If store employees didn't identify anyone,

Osborne would inform his boss, hold everyone, and await further instructions. Chee didn't like that. In fact, there was a lot of this duty he didn't like. For example, Agent Osborne's tight-lipped attitude about it. Well, he'd try again.

"If you were a gambling man, Oz, about what would be the odds this guy shows up in his Volks?" Chee asked. "Or has that credit card, if he does show up?"

Osborne was listening to some sort of music on his tape player headset. He reduced the volume, shrugged, said: "Very slim. Highly unlikely."

"Exactly," Chee said. "So having us out here waiting for this bird with damn little chance of seeing him is another of those things that tells me this Carl Mankin was either very important himself, or had done something very important."

Chee paused, glanced at Osborne. Osborne was listening, but pretending not to.

"I didn't see that name on your most-wanted list."

Osborne shrugged.

"If somebody stole my Discover Card, and I reported it missing—or if I disappeared myself,

hiding out, and was using it here and there—
would the federal government drop everything
and start this dragnet? I doubt it."

Osborne chuckled. "You think one of your
girlfriends would miss you?" he said. "How
about that pretty Officer Bernie Manuelito
you're always talking about. Would she come
back to look for you?"

Which caused Chee to change the subject of
his thoughts. He resumed his fruitless speculation about Bernie, about the real reasons she'd
quit the Navajo Tribal Police to become a
Border Patrol Officer, and about the letter from
her in his jacket pocket, what it had said about
the dangerous-sounding work she was doing,
and, worse, its absolute lack of any hint of missing him. But Chee didn't want to talk to Osborne
about Bernie. He let the remark pass and went
back to the question of Mankin.

"Or perhaps Mankin was in the act of doing
something very important for some very big bureaucrat," Chee said. "What do you think?"

"I don't think," Osborne said. "Remember?
You told me federal employees aren't allowed to
do that."

"Come on, Osborne," Chee said. "Someone

big in federal affairs believes this is important or we wouldn't even know about the credit card. The purchases were recent. Somebody big had to call Mr. Visa himself and get a drop-everything computer check made on that Mankin number. Right?"

"They don't tell me things like that."

"And they still haven't told you whether they've identified our well-dressed homicide victim? Right?"

Osborne nodded.

"Let me speculate then. Let's say the officially unidentified body and the Visa card both belong to Carl Mankin. And Mankin was either a much-trusted and highly ranked agent of something like the National Security Agency, or the Central Intelligence Agency, Drug Enforcement, or our new Homeland Security Agency, or any of the other ten or twelve federal intelligence bureaucracies busy competing with one another, and now his bosses have missed him. And they want to know who killed him? Or, more important, why?"

Osborne looked at Chee, yawned, and resumed staring out the window.

"So we're out here on the off chance that we

will catch whoever got off with Mankin's credit card, and he will tell us something useful." Chee said. "Is that it?"

"I wonder who started that notion that Navajos were silent, taciturn people," Osborne said. "My theory is the killer is the lead scout for a flying saucer invasion and he had to shoot Mankin because Mankin had uncovered their conspiracy to take over our planet? Or how about Carl Mankin is a favorite nephew of the president's best friend? That sound all right?" He turned off his tape player, fished another tape out of the glove box, and looked at it. "How about **James Taylor in Concert**? He's good."

"Whatever," Chee said. "You're the one who listens to it. And you know what I'm going to do tomorrow, if we're not still out here waiting for Volks? I'm going to a man I know who accepts Visa cards from his customers, give him this Mankin number, and get him to call Visa for a background check. Then I'll tell you, and you can pass it along to the top brass in the Bureau."

"I listen to the music to keep me from listening to you," Osborne said. "You'd finally wear me down and I'd be leaking all of our secrets."

So James Taylor's voice floated in, barely audible through the wrong side of Osborne's ear-phones, something about plans putting an end to someone catching Chee's attention. The plans someone made had permanently put an end to a still-unidentified well-dressed middle-aged man who might, or might not, be Carl Mankin. But whose plans? And what plans? And how did this fellow fit into them. Apparently not well because he'd been shot and then dumped facedown into a shallow wash and buried so ca-sually that the wind had blown the dirt away from one hand and the back of his head. A sad way to go into that next existence.

Osborne had removed his headphones to rub his ear just as James Taylor was remember-ing the lonely times when he could not find a friend. His sadness worsened Chee's mood. When his time came, Chee knew, his kin would come, and his friends. One of the Mormons in his paternal clan would suggest an undertaker, one of the born-again Christians in his maternal clan would agree, and the traditionals would po-litely ignore this. The designated one would wash his body, dress him properly, put his cere-monial moccasins on his feet, properly reversed to confuse any witch who might be hunting dead skin for his corpse powder bundle. Then his body would be carried to some secret place where no skinwalker could find it, no coyotes or ravens could reach it, no anthropologist could come to steal his little vial of pollen and his prayer jish to be stored in their museum basement. Then the sacred wind within him would begin its four-day journey into the Great Adventure that awaits us all.

Chee sighed.

Osborne took off his headset. "That Taylor stuff's too sad for you," he said. "You want something more upbeat? How about—"

Chee violated a traditional Navajo rule by interrupting.

"Look down there," he said. "I think I see our blue Volks van pulling up to the pumps at Huerfano Trading Post."

"OK," said Osborne, starting the engine. "Let's go talk to Carl Mankin."

"Or whoever stole his credit card."

It didn't seem to be Mankin. He had just finished hosing gasoline into his tank, a short man, burly, needing a shave, and wearing greasy coveralls. Probably part standard white man and part Jicarilla Apache. He was screwing on the gas tank cap when Osborne braked his Ford beside him. He glanced at Chee through a set of dark sunglasses, and then at Osborne, looking as if he expected to recognize them and surprised that he hadn't.

Osborne was out of the car, thrusting his FBI identification folder toward the man and asking him his identity.

Sunglasses took a step backward, startled. "Me? Why, I'm Delbert Chinosa."

"Could we see your credit card?" Chee asked.

"Credit card?" Chinosa was clearly startled by this confrontation. "What credit card?"

"The one you're holding there," said Osborne. "Let me see that."

"Well, now," Chinosa said. "It's not actually mine. I've got to give it back to my brother-in-law. But here." He handed the card to Osborne. A Visa, Chee noticed. Chinosa had taken off his sunglasses and was looking tense and uneasy.

Osborne examined the card and nodded to Chee.

"This card is made out to Carl Mankin," Osborne said. "You say you're not Carl Mankin. Is your brother-in-law Carl Mankin?"

"No sir. He's Albert Desboti. South of Dulce. I think this Mankin fella loaned it to him. Told him he could go ahead and use it."

Chinosa rubbed his hands on his coverall legs and managed a smile. "So Al told me I could go ahead and buy gas with it."

"At the pumps where you don't have to sign the credit card form," Osborne said. "Was that his idea?"

Chinosa managed another smile. "Said that would be all right. Said no harm in that."

"Well, not unless you're the one getting stuck with the expense," Osborne said. "And now we're all going to have to go find Albert Desboti."

They did, making the long drive into the Jicarilla Reservation; Chee with Chinosa guiding them in his van through the maze of dirt roads and past endless evidence that this famous oil and gas field was still producing its wealth of fossil fuel and Osborne following. Desboti seemed to have heard them coming. His little single-width mobile home was located on the east edge of Laguna Seca Mesa, and Desboti was standing in its door.

"Hey, Delbert," he shouted. "You just in time for supper." Then added something in Apache, which Chee interpreted as: "What you doing with that Navajo cop?"

Osborne was out of his sedan, flashing his

FBI credentials, introducing himself. Chinosa was saying he'd told them Desboti had loaned him the credit card.

"What credit card?" Desboti said. He grimaced.

"You're Albert Desboti?" Osborne said. "That correct?"

"That's right. Al Desboti."

Osborne displayed the Visa card. "You loan this to Mr. Chinosa?"

Desboti looked as though he didn't know how to answer that. He said: "What?"

Osborne laughed. "We're going to find out, one way or another. Why not just tell us about it. How'd you get the card. Save time."

"This Manley guy. He said use it if I need it. Just pay him back."

"It's Mankin," Osborne said. "Were you there when he was shot?"

"Shot?" Desboti's eyes were wide.

"Or were you the one who shot him?"

Chee had been leaning against Chinosa's van, watching Osborne work, thinking he was handling it fairly well, and maybe this blunt approach would save time. It did.

"I didn't shoot anybody," Desboti said, talking fast now. "I was cleaning up that campground. That's my job. For the tribal parks. And bears had smelled the food in the trash and turned over the canister. Scattered the stuff all around, and there it was on the ground with the garbage. Dirty, but a pretty good-looking billfold. I just picked it up and cleaned it off."

"Cleaned it off?"

Desboti grimaced again. "People come through here, they've saved up those damned paper diapers and they dump 'em out at the campgrounds."

"Oh," Osborne said, and glanced at Chee. It seemed to Chee that this answered a question for him. It made that trash bin a logical place to bury things you didn't want recovered.

"The credit card was in the wallet? What else?" Osborne asked.

"No money," Desboti said, looking thoughtful. Looking like he was trying to remember. "Nothing much. Driver's license. Two keys. Looked like car keys. Pretty empty, like it was new."

"You have it?"

Desboti opened his mouth, closed it, looked down, shrugged. Reached into his hip pocket and extracted a slim black leather wallet. "Just my stuff in it now," he said. He extracted what looked to Chee like a twenty and several small bills and handed it to Osborne.

He inspected it. Extracted two small padlock keys and showed them to Desboti. "These yours?"

"No. They were in it."

"Driver's license? Any other papers?"

"Well, yeah. There was a driver's license. And some cards. Insurance I think. And receipts you get at the gasoline pump. I think that was all." Desboti nodded, licked his lips. "Did you say somebody shot that man?"

"Yes," Osborne said. "Where are those other papers from the wallet."

"Went back into the trash with the baby diapers, then into the truck and off to the trash dump."

Chee closed his eyes. Osborne was going to say they'd go to that dump and Desboti was going to show them where he thought he dumped the load, and then they were going to start sorting through a mountain of dirty diapers, empty beer cans, and worse.

But Osborne didn't say anything for a long moment. Then he shrugged. "Let's go see exactly where you found this wallet."

Which, Chee thought, would be a waste of

time but far better than sifting through smelly diapers for the papers. And it was.

Driving back to Farmington through the summer darkness, Chee found himself beginning to form a fondness for Osborne. He steered the chat into telling Osborne about being sent by the Navajo Tribal Police back to a training session at the FBI Academy, comparing notes, relaxed and casual. "I still try to do those memory exercises they taught us. I can remember everything about that Jeep Cherokee rented to Mankin. How good are you?"

"I've lost some of it I guess. It was dirty white. Year-old model. Something over twenty-three thousand miles on it. Tires looked a little worse than that. Chip on the windshield. Lot of dirt and gravelly stuff on the floor pad. Lot of various tools in the back. Got it all written in my notes."

"I remember his copy of the rental form had him refusing the insurance, so forth," Chee said. "I think he put down some sort of oil-drilling outfit for his company."

"Got you there," Osborne said. "It was Seamless Weld."

"Oh, well," Chee said. "That could be pipeline maintenance. What did your boss say about Mankin? What he was doing up here? All that?"

"I don't know," Osborne said, looking grim. "We were told the El Paso office handled that."

"They didn't tell you what they found out? Boy! How can you work a case without that sort of information?"

Osborne didn't answer.

"Maybe you'll get it tomorrow," Chee said. "The fax machine broke."

"No," Osborne said. "I called down there and asked about it and the word was to cool it. Just find out who was using that credit card. Other people were handling the case and they'd be giving me my instructions."

"Be damned," Chee said. "That sounds funny."

"Funny? Yeah, I guess you could call it that." But his tone was bitter.

"I'll help you if I can," Chee said. "I'd presume our victim is the man who checked out that Hertz rental car left over by that pipeline pumping station—or whatever that contraption is. Match the prints in the car with the corpse and—"

"I'm sure that's all been done," Osborne said.

Chee said: "Was it—" and then cut off the questions. Why embarrass Osborne. It wasn't his fault. The FBI bureaucrats had always been notoriously inept. And now the word was that the Homeland Security law had laid another thick layer of political patronage on top of that— adding the chaos of a new power struggle to an already clogged system. Chee restarted his sentence. "Was it still my problem, I'd concentrate on that seven miles between where the car was left and where the body was dumped. Try to find somebody along that route who saw something. Then I'd look around the area he parked the car. There must be a reason they moved the body so far away from there. Killer shoots Mankin. His helper drives Mankin's car off to hide it."

"How about a better idea," Osborne said. "Why don't I just tell my supervisor if they won't give me the information I need to work with, then I say to hell with it and quit."

6

This windy afternoon was a sort of sad anniversary for Officer Bernadette Manuelito, and she was finding it tough to maintain her usual high level of cheerfulness. First the anniversary itself—six months since she had made the big decision—was confronting her with the thought that maybe she had made a horrible mistake in changing jobs and bidding good-bye to the Navajo Tribal Police and her family and friends (and Sergeant Jim Chee) to join the U.S. Customs Service.

A second damper on her spirits was the letter from Chee folded into a pocket of her U.S. Customs Service uniform. It was an infuriatingly ambiguous letter. So damned typical of Sergeant Chee. Third, was the uniform itself, the costume of the Customs Service Border

Patrol. New, stiff, and uncomfortable. She had felt much better, and looked better, in the NTP uniform she had cast aside.

Forth, and finally, there was the immediate cause of her discontent: she was lost.

Being lost was a new and unpleasant experience for Bernie. In the "Land Between the Sacred Mountains" of her Navajos, she knew the landscape by heart. Look east, the Turquoise Mountain rose against the sky. To the west, the Chuska Range formed the horizon. Beyond that the San Francisco Peaks were the landmark. South, the Zuñi Mountains. North, the La Platas. No need for a compass. No need for a map. But down here along the Mexican border all the mountains looked alike to her—dry, sawtoothed, and unfriendly.

The rough and rutted road on which she had parked her Border Patrol pickup also seemed unfriendly. Her U.S. Geological Survey map labeled it "primitive." Just ahead it divided. The left fork seemed to angle westward toward the Animas Mountains, and the right fork headed northward toward either the Hatchets or the Little Hatchets. The map indicated no such fork. It showed the track continuing westward toward the little New Mexico village of Rodeo (now her home), where it connected with an asphalt road running toward Douglas, Arizona.

The map was old, probably obsolete, obviously wrong. Bernie folded it. She'd take the right fork. It had the advantage of reducing the chance she wander across the Mexican border into the great emptiness of the Sonoran Desert, run out of gasoline, and into the custody of Mexican police, thereby becoming an illegal immigrant herself.

Fifteen minutes and eight miles later she stopped again where her track topped a rocky ridge. She would base her judgment on the reality as seen through her binoculars and not on a USGS survey, which probably was made when General Pershing was fighting Pancho Villa's army ninety years ago.

Bernie leaned against the front fender and scanned the horizon. It was hot—a hundred and one yesterday and about the same today. The usual August thunderheads were building to the south and west. The heat haze shimmered over the rolling desert, making it hard to know exactly what one was seeing. Nothing much to see, anyway, Bernie thought, if you didn't know which of those ragged peaks was where. But miles to the north she saw a glitter of reflected light. A windshield? It disappeared in the shimmer. But then she saw a plume of dust. Probably a truck and apparently not far to the west of where this track would take her.

Bernie climbed back into her pickup. She'd catch the truck and learn what it was doing out here. After all that was her job, wasn't it? Maybe it would be operated by a "coyote" smuggling in a load of illegal aliens or bundles of coke. Probably not, since Ed Henry had told her they almost always operate at night. And Henry, being the Customs officer more or less in temporary charge of the Shadow Wolves tracking unit and an old-timer in this desolate section of border land, probably knew what he was talking about. Nice guy, Henry. Friendly, down to earth. One of those men totally confident in himself. Nothing like Sergeant Chee, whom she had left behind just six months ago. Chee tried to play the role of an experienced shift commander of the Navajo Tribal Police, but Chee wasn't so sure of himself. And it showed. In some ways he was like a little boy. Didn't know what to say to her, for example. Which brought her back to the letter in her pocket, which she didn't want to think about.

So she thought about being lost instead.

Whoever was making the dust could probably tell her where she was.

She caught up to the vehicle just west of a long ridge of volcanic rock that Bernie had decided might be part of either the Brockman Hills or the Little Hatchet Mountains. It was parked at the bottom of the brushy hump she was crossing—a green panel truck towing a small green trailer. It had stopped at a gate in a fence that seemed to run endlessly across the arid landscape. Across the fence a pickup sat. Bernie parked and got out her binoculars.

Two men at the gate, one with a mustache, wearing what looked to Bernie like some sort of military fatigue uniform and a long-billed green "gimme" cap. The other's face was shaded by the typical wide-brimmed, high-crowned straw favored by those fated to work under the desert sun. This one was unlocking the gate, hanging the padlock on the wire, pulling the gate open. The green trailer, she noticed, wore a Mexican license plate.

Bernie picked up her camera, rolled down the side window. She had eight unexposed frames on a roll of thirty-six, the others being mostly portraits of tire tracks, shoe prints, and other evidence that either man or beast had passed through the empty landscape. Those Henry would examine and use to lecture her on what she needed to learn to become a competent tracker. This one would just prove to Henry that she was already keeping an eye on what was going on. She put on the long lens and focused. The gate was open now. Straw Hat stood beside it. Green Cap had a hand on his open truck door and stared up the road at her. Bernie took the picture. Green Cap said something to Straw Hat, pointed toward her, laughed, climbed into his truck. Straw Hat waved him through the gate.

Bernie started her truck, gunned it down the slope as fast as the rocky ruts allowed, and turned off the "primitive" road she had been following onto the lane that led into the gate—producing a cloud of dust. Straw Hat had relocked his gate and stood behind it. He removed the hat, fanned away the dust, and replaced it.

"Young lady, it's way too hot to be in such a hurry," he said. "What's the rush?"

Bernie leaned out the window.

"I'll need you to unlock that gate for me," she said. "I want to see what that man's hauling."

"Well, I guess I could help you with that."

Straw Hat was grinning at her, a tall, lanky, long-faced man. "Save you some time and bad roads to cross. He's not transporting no wetbacks. Not a thing of any possible interest to you folks. Just a bunch of construction gear."

"Well, thank you, sir," Bernie said. "But my boss is going to insist that I should have gone on in and seen for myself."

Straw Hat didn't respond to that.

"Just doing my job," Bernie added. She made a dismissive gesture. "United States Border Patrol."

"My name's O'day," Straw Hat said. "Tom." He raised his right hand in the "glad to meet you" gesture.

"Bernadette Manuelito—Officer Manuelito today, and while we're talking, the man I want to see about is getting away."

"Trouble is," said Tom O'day, "I can't let you in here." He pointed to the No Trespassing sign mounted to the gate post with NO ADMISSION WITHOUT WRITTEN PERMISSION printed under it. "You got to have a note from the fella that owns this place. That or get him to call out here and arrange to get the gate unlocked."

"I'm an agent of the Border Patrol," Bernie said. "Federal officer."

"I noticed the uniform," O'day said. "Noticed that decal on your truck." O'day was grinning at her. "So if you will just show me your search warrant, or a note from my boss, then I'll unlock the gate and in you go."

Bernie considered this a moment. None of this was seeming very criminal to her. However—

"Hot pursuit," she said. "How about that? Then I don't need a search warrant."

Now it became O'day's time to ponder. "It didn't seem much like hot pursuit from what I saw of it," he said. "Except for the dust you was raising. Trouble is the owner of this spread is tough as hell about keeping people out." He shrugged. "Had some vandalism."

"Vandalism?" She gestured at the landscape. "You mean like tourists breaking off the cactus pods or the snake weed. Or getting off with some of the rocks?"

Tom O'day seemed to be enjoying this exchange. He chuckled. "Somebody did cut some of our fencing wire once," he said, "but that was some years ago, back before Old Man Brockman decided to sell the place and Ralph Tuttle got it. Now it's his boy, Jacob, running it. But I think maybe some corporation or such actually put up the money. And young Jacob, he's always away somewhere or other enjoying himself."

"Brockman?" Bernie said. "That the man they named that range of hills after?"

"I think that was his granddaddy," O'day said.

Bernie had been staring through the windshield, nervously watching the last sign of dust left by the green pickup disappearing.

"Tell you what," she said. "I'm going to declare that I am in hot pursuit of a subject suspected of smuggling illegal aliens—or maybe we'll call it controlled substances—and I ordered you to unlock the gate or face the full force and majesty of federal law. Would that do it?"

O'day tilted back his hat. They stared at each other.

"Well, yes," he said. "I think Mr. Jacob Tuttle would buy that. I may need you to swear that there were no ibexes or orxys or even pronghorn antelope in view, and that I confirmed you didn't have a hunting rifle with you."

O'day was unlocking the gate, swinging it open.

"Ibex?" Bernie asked. "The African antelope

with the long horns? I thought the game department quit importing them."

"That's the oryx you were describing. The ibex is the goat out of the Morocco mountains. And, yeah, the game department decided importing them wasn't worth the effort, but Tuttle wanted his friends to have African safaris without making the long trip. That's what that big expensive fence is about."

"To keep them in?"

O'day was grinning at her. "And keep you poachers out."

Bernie drove her pickup through.

"Hold it a minute. I want to close this and then I'll show you where he'll be. It's just about three miles but it's easy to get lost."

Bernie had no doubt of that. O'day locked the gate, climbed into his truck, and headed down the tracks the green pickup had left.

By Bernie's odometer it was a fraction less than four miles before she passed a taller than usual cluster of cacti and saw the truck with the green trailer parked with two other trucks—a flatbed and one towing a horse trailer. She had lagged far enough behind O'day's pickup to avoid breathing his dust, but close enough to see he had done some talking on his cell phone during the trip. Probably telling any illegals who might be where they were headed that a cop was coming.

Three men were standing by the trucks as O'day drove up, apparently waiting. Fat chance of her seeing anything they didn't want her to see. But then if they were smuggling illegals, where could they have hidden them?

O'day opened her truck door, inviting her out.

"Here we are," he said. "And here is your smuggler. Colonel Abraham Gonzales of Seamless Welds Incorporated. And Mr. Gonzales, this young lady is Officer Manuelito of the U.S. Border Patrol."

Gonzales bowed, tipped his cap, said: **"Con mucho gusto, Señorita,"** and produced one of those smiles that men of Gonzales's age often display when meeting appealing young women. The side flaps of the trailer behind him were down, and Bernie could see racks of tools, pipes, hoses, and something that she guessed might be a motor of some sort—perhaps an air compressor, pump, or something. Beyond the trailer stood a much-weathered shack, its single room roofed and sided with corrugated metal sheeting, and its door hanging open. Beside the shack was a metal watering tank, and past it three workmen stood beside a front-end loader parked beside the shack, occupied with looking at her. If she wanted to collect illegals, Bernie thought, at least two of those probably would qualify. Definitely the youngest one with the mustache now giving her a younger version of the Gonzales smile. His was the "come on, baby" leer.

Gonzales gestured toward the open side of his trailer. "No place in here to haul illegals," he said. "But you're welcome to take a look."

"OK," Bernie said. "But actually I misread your license plate. I thought it was a Canadian truck and maybe you were smuggling in maple syrup, or something like that."

Gonzales considered that a moment and laughed. So did O'day, but his seemed genuine.

"I doubt if Mr. Gonzales has anything illegal in that trailer," he said. "But maybe you ought to look. And I've got to get this crew back to work."

"Doing what?" Bernie asked, walking to the trailer. "What are you building? Or digging?"

"We're going to set up that windmill," O'day said, pointing to a pile of framework beside the shack. "Going to have a little oasis here. Water tanks for the livestock and a place for Mr. Tuttle's pets to get a drink."

"Oryxs. Right? I'd like to see one of those."

"Just take a look," he said. "That's a couple of them over yonder." He pointed east toward the hills. "They're waiting for us to go away so they can come in and see if there's anything in the tank for them to drink. Trouble is, it's about dry. We're going to try to fix that."

"Where are they?" Bernie said. "Oh, I see them now. Wow. Bigger than I expected. Aren't they a kind of antelope?"

"African antelope," O'day said. "One of Tuttle's hunting buddies shot one out here last spring. Weighed over four hundred pounds."

Bernie finished a cursory check of the tools on the trailer's racks, the welding masks, propane tanks, compressor engine, and a lot of large machinery far beyond her comprehension. She nodded to Gonzales. "Thank you. I don't often get a chance to meet colonels."

Gonzales looked slightly abashed. "Retired," he said. "And from one of the Mexican army's less noted reserve regiments."

O'day was grinning at her. "That about do it?"

"I think so," she said. "What's the best way from here to get to . . ." Bernie paused, visualizing her map, looking for a place that should be fairly nearby and also on a regular marked road that actually went somewhere. "To get to Hatchita."

"First I got to let you back through the gate. From there you—hell, I'll show you when we get there."

"First I want to get a picture of those oryx," Bernie said. She reached into her truck and extracted the camera. "No harm shooting them with a camera is there?"

O'day stared out at the animals, still waiting on the hillside. "Kinda far away," he said. "They'll just be specks."

"I've got a telescopic lens," she said, tapping it, and got into her truck. "But I'll drive a little ways up the hill there to get a better shot."

"Well, now," he said, looking doubtful.

"Just a few hundred yards," Bernie said, starting the engine. "I want to get where I won't have all this clutter in the picture. Make it look like I shot it in the wilds of Africa."

That seemed to satisfy O'day, but when she stopped a quarter mile up the hill he was still watching her. She focused on the largest oryx, which also seemed to be staring at her. Then she got another shot of Gonzales, also staring, and of his van, the shack, and the equipment around it. Why waste those last exposures on a thirty-six-frame roll?

O'day pointed her way through what he called "Hatchet Gap," which led her to a road that actually had been graded and graveled, and on to County Road 9, and thence to Hatchita and the turn south toward Interstate Highway 10 and Eleanda's little house in Rodeo. Straight road now, no traffic. She extracted Jim Chee's letter from her jacket pocket. She spread it on the steering wheel and zipped through the introductory paragraphs to the terminal portion.

We now have a case that would interest you. It's a very professional-looking homicide with the victim shot once in the back from a distance. Well-dressed man and I don't mean by Farmington standards. Tailored shirt, even. Osborne said even the shoes were custom made. He was found out in the Checkboard Rez just south of Jicarilla Apache land. He was in an El Paso rent-a-

car parked on the track leading to one of those Giant Oil pump stations and there was a bunch of stuff about welding and pipeline fixing, etc., in the car which didn't seem to fit with the way he was dressed. No identification on him, but the car rental papers showed it had been signed to a welding/metal construction company down in Mexico. Now Osborne tells me the case has all of a sudden been taken away from the regional FBI, and he thinks it's being run right out of Washington.

I'm hoping it will involve Customs violations in some way or another and maybe that would give me an excuse to get down there and look into it, and invite you out to dinner.

Sincerely,
Jim

Bernie made a face, refolded the letter back into her pocket.

"And sincerely to you, too, Sergeant Chee," she said to the windshield, feeling sour, dusty, and exhausted. But by the time she saw the little cluster of buildings that formed Rodeo, she was thinking about the Mexican welding/metal construction connection. She'd want to talk about this with Mr. Henry. Make sure she knew what sort of checking she should do to find out if that famous North American Free Trade Agreement made all such traffic free and easy. And she'd want to talk with Jim Chee about the welding/metal construction company renting the car for his homicide victim.

7

Former Lieutenant Joe Leaphorn, now retired, had his day pretty well planned. Professor Louisa Bourbonette was up on the Ute Reservation collecting her oral histories from the tribe's elderly. She had left even earlier than usual, the sky visible through his east-facing window barely showing predawn pink when her bumping around in her bedroom awakened him.

He listened to the sound of her car fading, felt a twinge of loneliness, and considered for a moment bringing up the topic of marriage again, and then dismissed the idea. She'd tell him, as she always did, that she had tried that once and didn't care for it. That would be followed by a few days of uneasiness between them and of his feeling a vague sort of guilt for even thinking of trying to replace Emma. The infection had killed her physically, but Emma lived on in his mind. Emma would always be his lover. But Louisa had become a confidante and a friend. He was smart enough to see she cared for him, and the sentiment was mutual.

Hearing Louisa drive away left a sort of silence that made him remember too much. He had planned to use the quiet time to exercise his mind—gone rusty with retirement idleness. He'd accumulated a list of nine really tough Free Cell games he'd had to abandon unsolved on his computer. He consumed his breakfast coffee and toast, turned on his machine, called up game 1192, and was planning his first move when the telephone rang.

"Dan Mundy, Joe," the voice said. "How's retirement treating you? You keeping busy?"

Mundy, Joe thought. Yes. Prosecutor in the U.S. Attorney's Office. Old-timer. Retired years ago.

"Can't complain," Leaphorn said. "How about you?"

"I'm bored with it," Mundy said. "You doing anything important today?"

"Working on a puzzle on my computer."

"How about me coming by? I want to intro-
duce you to a fellow."

Leaphorn had been retired long enough to
know that when such casual semifriends called it
was always to ask a favor. But why not? Perhaps
it would offer some variety. Anyway, what could
he say?

Joe said: "OK. I'll have some coffee made."

Mundy looked exactly as Leaphorn had remembered him. White hair, sharp blue eyes, precisely
clipped goatee. "Joe," he said. "This is Jason
Ackerman. Known him since we both cribbed
our way through law school. But he's still prac-
ticing. Big office in Washington. Jase, this is
Lieutenant Joe Leaphorn, retired. Out here they
call him the 'Legendary Lieutenant.' I've told
you about him."

Jason shifted the briefcase he'd been holding
to his left hand and offered Leaphorn the right
one. With the hand shaking done, Leaphorn
motioned his visitors to sit and brought in
Louisa's tray with its array of saucered cups,
sugar bowl, creamer, spoons, and napkins.
Coffee was poured, pleasantries exchanged.

"And now," Leaphorn said. "What brings you to Window Rock?"

This produced a moment of hesitation, a sipping of coffee by Mundy. Ackerman was waiting for him to answer.

"I guess officially and formally, it's none of our business. We're just being nosey," Mundy said. "But we're sort of curious about that murder case. That fellow shot up there just off the southwest edge of the Jicarilla Reservation."

"Which murder case?"

Mundy laughed, shook his head. "Come on, Joe. You don't have that many."

"You mean the recent one? Victim unidentified?"

"And why wasn't he identified?" Mundy asked. "I heard he got there in a rental car. They don't let those cars go without knowing who they're renting them to. That should be easy to track."

"So I'd think," Leaphorn said. He sampled his own coffee. "You know I'm retired now. It's not my business."

Ackerman shifted his briefcase in his lap. "We'd like to make it your business," he said, smiling at Leaphorn.

"Now I'm curious," Leaphorn said. "Why would you want to do that?"

"We need to know more about that case," Mundy said.

Leaphorn was beginning to enjoy this sparring. "Like what? Why would that be?"

"Two different reasons," Mundy said. "You're familiar with the trouble the Interior Department is in now. With both the Federal Appeals Court and the House Investigations folks getting interested in what happened to that Tribal Trust Fund royalty money."

"Sure," Leaphorn said. "The four-billion-dollar question. Or was it forty billion?"

"The Congressional Accounting Office says it's closer to forty," Mundy said, "and the new suit the tribal attorneys just filed says the government owes 'em a hundred and thirty-seven million dollars. That was starting to emerge when I was retiring and it got to be a serious thing with me. Somebody must have been making off with that royalty money. Or more likely, the oil and gas companies, or the pipeline people, just weren't paying it at all. I wanted to know who, and how the cheating was handled. I still do."

"Me too," Leaphorn said. "I wish I could tell you."

"We think you could help."

"I'll try by giving you my opinion. I think if you're going to find the answer you'll find it by sorting through about fifty years of paperwork in Interior Department and Bureau of Indian Affairs offices back in Washington. And then you hire about a hundred more auditors and do the same thing with the books of a bunch of coal companies, copper companies, oil companies, pipeline companies, natural gas outfits, and . . . Who am I leaving out?"

Ackerman was looking impatient. He cleared his throat.

"Mr. Leaphorn is right about that, of course," Ackerman said. "But we think something connected with that problem must have been going on out here. Maybe part of the puzzle is here. Maybe not. But we'd like to know what."

Leaphorn felt another increase in his interest in this visit, this one sharp.

"Connected? This sounds like you think this homicide fits into that. How could that be?"

"We're hoping you could find out some things that would tell us that," Ackerman said.

"We think maybe somebody has a lot to gain, probably politically, by finding out what happened to that royalty money, and who got it, and so forth. And they were checking into that, and somebody who didn't want the secret out shot the fellow they had looking into it for them."

"Let's see now," Leaphorn said. "First thing you'd need to know is the identity of the victim. The FBI has his fingerprints, of course, and the prints on the rental vehicle. I'd say the Bureau has him named. Apparently the Bureau is not releasing that. Could I find out why not? I can't see how I could out here at Window Rock. It suggests our victim was well connected—one way or another. Can you get all that?"

Mundy said, "You mean find out this dead guy's identity. And who he was working for?" He looked at Ackerman. Ackerman shrugged, nodded.

Mundy said, "Probably. I'm sure we can find out his identity. Who he was. But who he was working for? That wouldn't be so easy."

"So what do you think I can do?"

"Find out what he was doing here. What he was looking for. Was he finding anything. Who he was talking to. What sort of questions he was asking them."

Ackerman cleared his throat. "Everything he was asking about."

Leaphorn considered this. "I'll get you a refill," he said. He went into the kitchen, emerged with the coffeepot, and poured.

"Now it's time for you to tell the name of this murder victim and those little details that would make it possible to do anything for you. Start with the identification."

Ackerman looked at Mundy.

"We don't have the name yet," said Mundy. "But I can get it for you in a day or two."

Leaphorn gestured toward his telephone. "You can call from here."

Mundy laughed. "Joe. I have to do this very quietly. You know how the Bureau can be out here. Well, in Washington it's a lot worse. Somebody pretty big seems to be sitting on this homicide case. That's one of the things we're trying to learn. Who is the Bureau covering for."

"Who do you think?"

Mundy glanced at Ackerman, who managed an almost imperceptible nod.

"Three possibilities on our list. One is a very senior U.S. senator who sits on a crucial subcommittee. Another is also a VIP heavy hitter on the Republican side of the aisle. Another is a distinguished and well-advertised corporation that has had huge holdings in the energy industry. Oil. Gas. Pipelines. Coal. Electricity."

Leaphorn considered that a moment.

"If somebody hired our murder victim to dig up evidence for them, what would be their motive? Evidence of what?"

Ackerman sighed. "Maybe evidence to use in an election campaign. Proving the incumbent was a crook. Maybe evidence to blackmail a chief executive officer. Maybe . . . all sorts of uses for knowledge." Ackerman laughed. "As is said in Washington, 'Knowledge is power.'"

"I'll tell you what," Leaphorn said. "Get me the identity and everything else you can learn about our homicide victim and I'll see if I can learn anything. But don't count on it."

8

Professor Louisa Bourbonette got involved more or less by accident. Chee had called the home of retired lieutenant Joe Leaphorn in Window Rock. Louisa had answered. Moved in with Joe until she finished her Southern Ute oral history research, she said, or until fall semester enrollment time at NAU, or until Leaphorn got tired of her cooking. Chee said he'd like to talk to Leaphorn if the Legendary Lieutenant was available. Louisa said she expected him in about an hour and could Leaphorn call Chee at his place in Shiprock? Chee said he was at the Navajo Tribal Police headquarters in Window Rock. Good, said Louisa. Why not just come over and join us for lunch.

He had. Thus a nonpolice viewpoint, feminine and academic, was introduced into Jim

Chee's complex problem. On the surface, it involved what he should do about an obviously touchy murder case and what Leaphorn thought he should do, if anything, about some funny business he seemed to be finding out about a welding company. Most of all it concerned Bernie Manuelito's vague connection with all this, and Bernie herself.

Chee had wanted this conversation to be very simple. He would explain his law enforcement puzzle with his former supervisor, seek his opinion on what caused an apparently unusually fierce federal interest in a Visa card, and so forth. He hoped to arouse Leaphorn's interest and thus lead the Legendary Lieutenant into using his famed legendary network of good old boy cops to get some questions answered. Finally, and most important, he wanted to tell Leaphorn about a letter he'd received from Bernie this morning. It had included some photos that were not only worrisome, but might offer a legitimate reason for Chee to send himself down into New Mexico's bootheel to visit Bernie. It seemed to Chee that having Professor Bourbonette listening in on that would be sort of embarrassing.

But even as he was thinking this, the aroma

of roasting lamb chops reached him from the kitchen. A prospect of a decent meal made this possible complication easy to tolerate.

"It's true," Leaphorn was saying. "We're finally getting the thunderheads and the lightning, but the rains are way overdue. Anyway, I'll bet weather's not what you're thinking about."

"Well, no," Chee said.

"I'd guess it's that homicide you had up in the Checkerboard Reservation. You have an identification yet of the victim?"

Chee laughed. "I don't. But if his name isn't Carl Mankin, then we have two crimes instead of one. I was hoping you'd tell me what's being talked about by your law enforcement friends over the morning doughnuts."

Leaphorn looked surprised. He was sitting in his living room recliner, feet on the ottoman, TV on but just a background murmur. Now Leaphorn leaned forward and clicked off the set, looked at Chee, said: "They haven't told you yet?"

"Nope."

"Well, now," Leaphorn said. "That's interesting, isn't it?"

Chee nodded. "Told me what?"

"Well, I hear the victim was shot in the back. He was well dressed. No identification on him.

Body left in the sage few yards from one of those dirt oil field roads. No vehicle around. Then a few days later, I heard the case was taken away from the Gallup and Farmington agents—not to Albuquerque and Phoenix, but all the way to Washington. A little later I heard the Jicarilla Apache cops had found a rented car abandoned somewhere on their reservation and took some prints off of it. Then the federals wouldn't tell them whether or not the prints matched anybody. That about right?"

Chee nodded. "Pretty close. Except when I called Dulce about it, they gave me Sergeant Dungae, and he said the car seemed to have been wiped down and they just got some marginal partials here and there."

Leaphorn took off his glasses, rubbed his eyes, and shook his head. "Guy named Ed Franklin used to be supervising agent out here. I think he was before your time. He told me that old J. Edgar Hoover used to tell his people, 'Knowledge is power and be damn careful who you share it with.' Who are you working with? You getting the silent treatment?"

"His name's Osborne," Chee said. "And actually, he's pretty good. I think he's been told to be . . . uh, let's call it discreet. I doubt if he knows much more than I do. For example, both the credit card and the rental car connect to an outfit in El Paso. But the El Paso FBI office isn't telling Osborne what they found out about Mankin there."

Leaphorn made a wry face.

Chee described the stakeout at the Huerfano Trading Post and the adventures with the credit card. "I figured Washington must have had an eye on this card number or those purchases wouldn't have been caught so fast. Osborne wouldn't talk about it."

"Probably they haven't told him either," Leaphorn said. He considered this a moment, shook his head. "What I hear is that the top Bureau people in Albuquerque and Phoenix were sort of encouraged to quit asking about the identity of the dead fellow. The gossips say they were told to lose interest in whose prints were on the car, about who picked up the body at the morgue. Told just to work on other cases. Washington would handle this one."

Chee nodded.

"That doesn't seem to surprise you," Leaphorn said. He laughed. "I didn't really think it would."

"I went to First National in Farmington.

Have an account there," Chee said. Asked a cashier friend to check on a Visa card held by Carl Mankin. Gave him the number and all that. He called me the next day, asked me what the hell I was getting him into. About two hours after he made the inquiry an FBI agent showed up at his office. He wanted to know why he was asking about Mankin's card."

"And then the FBI came to see you?"

Now Chee chuckled. "They didn't have to. It was Osborne. He knew exactly what I was up to."

"Pretty slick," Leaphorn said, looking somber.

"What do you mean?"

"I mean you knew that if that Visa inquiry call rattled the federal chains in Washington it would confirm your suspicions."

"Which ones?"

Leaphorn held up a finger. "First, that the body left in the sage brush was the fellow who owned the credit card dumped way over there on the Jicarilla Reservation. And, second, that some sort of cover-up was going on."

Chee made a deprecatory face. "Circumstantial evidence, anyway. But what's being covered up?"

"I'd call it awfully strong circumstantial evidence," Leaphorn said. He was frowning, leaning forward in his chair. "They'll have checked that wallet you found for prints by now. Osborne wouldn't tell you if they found any that matched the body?"

"I doubt they told Osborne," Chee said, aware that Professor Bourbonette had been standing in the kitchen doorway, listening to all this. "It's not Osborne's case any longer," he said, sort of explaining it to her. Then laughed. "It never was Chee's case."

"Are you gentlemen ready to join me for lunch?" she asked, stood aside, and invited them to the table. "You haven't asked my opinion," Louisa said as she sat down, "but if you had I would recommend to Jim that he just be happy Great White Father in Washington wants to do his work for him. And Joe should be happy he's retired and it's none of his business."

"Come on, Louisa," Leaphorn said. "Don't tell me you're not curious about this. Who is this homicide victim? Why the secrecy?"

"Can I guess? He was a special agent looking into something politically touchy. Instead of having a media circus about his assassination out here, raising all sorts of questions, the U.S.

Attorney General decides just to ship him home, have the proper people announce that he died suddenly of stroke, and funeral services will be held next week."

"Could be," Leaphorn said. "But how about the hard part. What was the touchy business he was looking into?"

Louisa considered that a moment while she passed the pepper shaker to Chee.

"How about that big lawsuit some of the tribes are filing against the Department of the Interior, claiming the Bureau of Indian Affairs has been stealing from their trust fund since about 1880?"

"You wouldn't find any clues to that out here," Leaphorn said. "You'd be digging into dusty filing cabinets in accounting offices. Stuff like that. The stealing was probably done in the way oil and natural gas—and maybe coal— was accounted when it was taken from tribal lands."

"Maybe he was checking records out here," Chee said. "His body was found out in oil and gas territory."

Louisa welcomed this support with a nod. "And don't forget that the Four Corners field is the biggest source of natural gas in North America. Billions of bucks going down the pipelines."

Chee swallowed a bite of lamb chop and cut off another. "Maybe this guy was looking for ways the gas gauges are fixed to record the right kind of misleading information," he said. "Maybe he found it."

This produced a thoughtful silence. Chee extracted Bernie's letter from his pocket.

"From Bernie Manuelito," he said, and spread the photos she'd sent on the table. "She's with the Border Patrol now, learning how to track illegals."

"Joe told me about that," Louisa said, giving Chee a look that was both curious and sympathetic. "I'll bet you miss her."

Chee, not knowing exactly what to say, said: "Bernie was a good cop," and pushed the most interesting picture toward Leaphorn. "She said she took this on that old Brockman Ranch, way down south of Lordsburg. Rich guy named Tuttle bought it. He's trying to get a herd of North African mountain goats started down there. Ibex, I think they are. Or maybe oryx."

Leaphorn studied it. Louisa was examining

another one. "Some of them on the slope here," she said. "Oryx is right, but they're not goats. They're a breed of antelope."

"What am I looking for in this?" Leaphorn asked.

"Notice the sign on the trailer behind the truck. 'Seamless Welds.'"

"Yeah. I see it."

"Our homicide victim listed El Paso Seamless Welds as his company on the rental agreement," Chee said.

Leaphorn looked at the photo again, said: "Well, now," and handed it to Louisa.

"Another thing about this, I did some checking and called the Seamless Weld company in El Paso. The guy they referred me to there said they didn't have anyone working named Mankin. Hadn't rented him a car."

Another thoughtful silence. Louisa broke it.

"I'm thinking that if Joe had his map here he'd be measuring the distance from that exotic animal ranch to where you found the rented car," she said. "A couple of hundred miles, I guess, and he'd be drawing a line between them, and another line back to Washington, and trying to make some connections."

"I don't know," Leaphorn said. "But I think I'd call Bernie about the car rental agreement and Seamless Weld."

"I will," Chee said.

Professor Bourbonette smiled at him. "I think you should drive down there and discuss it with her."

9

When Customs Service District Supervisor Ed Henry was a seventh grader in Denver he'd found a way intelligence and technical skills could augment income. His mother gave him a daily quarter for the pay phone at the bus stop outside Aspen Middle School. He'd call her at the laundry where she worked. If her duties kept her overtime, he'd take the city bus home and get supper started. Otherwise he'd do his homework at the bus stop until she picked him up.

To Henry this phone call had seemed a needless expense. Henry avoided it by drilling a hole through his quarter in shop class and threading a copper wire through it. With practice, he perfected the system. Drop the quarter in the slot, hear the sound of it being registered, then quickly pull it out for repeated use.

At first this merely saved Henry his quarters. But when another kid saw what he was doing, Henry used the same system to give the boy a free call. From that came the idea of cashing in on his wait beside the telephone booth, serving other students who showed up to call home. Henry charged a dime per call, thereby saving the customer fifteen cents.

When Henry's mother inquired about his new affluence he explained it. She rated it questionable, but as only American Telephone and Telegraph was the loser, her only instruction to Ed was to be careful, keep his mouth shut, and not overdo it.

An academic scholarship took Ed Henry to a smallish college in one of those Texas counties that continued to prohibit alcoholic beverages under the state's local option law. Telephones there made the coin-recovery business impossible, but it was far more profitable to drive his old car across the county line, fill the whiskey orders from fraternity and sorority students, and deliver the bottles to prearranged hiding places under bushes. Following his mother's "be careful" advice, Henry had discreetly approached the appropriate police captain and arranged a system of splitting the profits. That plan left him enough to make his car payments and send a little home to augment his mother's income—which was failing along with her health.

This eventually led Ed Henry to the U.S. Customs Service, the Border Patrol, and to where he sat in his office this particular morning going through the personnel file of Bernadette Manuelito, his newest charge, and wondering if he had any reason to be worried about her. His mother's stroke had forced Henry to drop out of college, but his flawless performance of his end of the deal with the police captain had earned him an enthusiastic recommendation from the captain to a friend in a Denver area juvenile detention system. Henry became a reformatory officer, moved from that to a sheriff's deputy job, and from that to the Customs Service—each time helped along by recommendations from superiors who appreciated his diligence, his intelligence, his reliability, and his talent for getting along with everyone. As the sheriff had said in his letter to Customs Service: "Mr. Henry honestly likes people. He enjoys helping folks and it pays off in their cooperation."

Which was true. Ed Henry liked Bernadette Manuelito from the very first, an intelligent, levelheaded young woman a bit like his own daughter. She had a lot to learn about border patrolling, but she would learn fast, being energetic and eager. Maybe a wee bit too eager, Ed Henry was thinking. His bedside telephone had rung just a few minutes after seven A.M., which would be just a little after nine in Washington, or maybe New York. It was The Man, and The Man had sounded grim.

"Henry," he said, "why was one of your people out on the Tuttle Ranch?"

"What?" Henry had said, trying to get himself fully awake, trying to figure out what this was about. "I didn't send an agent out there."

"Woman cop with Border Patrol credentials. Woman named Manuelito. She was following Gonzales and she took a bunch of pictures. Tell me why."

All Henry could tell The Man was that Bernie was a new recruit in the Shadow Wolf tracking unit and he'd sent her into the boot heel territory to try her hand at picking up some trails the illegals had been using. That did not please The Man.

"I'll call you back in three hours at your office number. I want you to tell me then why she was following Gonzales and why she was taking pictures and what her connections are. And get those pictures and see to it that they get to me."

"I can tell you she's a Navajo. Had been with the Navajo Tribal Police and—" Henry stopped. The line was dead.

"That son of a bitch," Henry said. He sat on his bed, floor cool under his bare feet, wondering just what The Man looked like. He knew him only by his voice, and heard that rarely since his connection in this sideline job was the very polite fellow from Juarez who called himself Carlos Delo and who had showed Henry how he could augment his income on the border as efficiently as he had in college. Delo seemed to get his instructions from the East Coast voice, passed the word along when a favor was needed from Henry, and arranged deposits in an El Paso bank account later.

Henry had heard the voice only three times before, always at moments of some sort of crisis, but he recognized it instantly: the effete East Coast intellectual sound—the Kennedy broad "a," the softness at the wrong places. Henry had pictured him as having a sort of long, narrow, British royalty face, thin lips, neatly coifed white hair. A bank official, probably, with a limo waiting for him about forty floors below, calling some low-level flunkey in New Mexico just to make sure a loan he'd signed off on was being protected. Well—

The telephone rang. Henry looked at it, grimaced, picked it up, and said: "Yes."

"You're going to get a call from The Man," this voice said. It was the clipped, precise sound of Charley Delo. "He is pissed off."

"What's going on?"

"Henry, you know they don't tell me, and I don't ask 'em. They tell me what to do, and I do it. And if I need some help from you, I tell you what I need. That's how we make a living."

"Who is that arrogant son of a bitch? I see him as a very important loan officer in a very lofty bank and he's overseeing an export-import business that wouldn't have Customs Service approval."

"I don't know, and you don't want to know. All I know is he doesn't want Customs cops messing around out there around the Brockman Hills. He wants you to make sure they won't."

"I told him I didn't send anyone out there."

"You need to get hold of that woman Customs Officer and find out what the hell she was doing, and get those pictures to me. Get 'em to the bank in Juarez and leave them in our safety deposit box. He also wants a picture of that woman cop."

Henry held the telephone away from his ear and rubbed his forehead. "Hey," the voice was saying. "Hey. You there."

"Yeah," Henry said.

"You hear what I said."

"Yes," Henry said. "I heard you."

10

Customs Officer Bernadette Manuelito was driving west on Interstate Highway 10, heading toward the intersection with State Road 146, when her telephone beeper distracted her. She intended to take 146 south to the village of Hatchita, where 146, for no reason she could discern, became State Road 81, and stay on 81 until it met the Mexican border. Judging from her map, she could see it simply ended there. Bernie's goal was to continue following supervisor Henry's instructions.

"First thing to do is get acquainted with the boot heel section of New Mexico," Henry had said. "And while you're doing that, see if you're smart enough to find the Hoe-ches Highway."

That was the Border Patrol's jocular title for the footpaths used by illegals in filtering across from Mexico, and all Henry told her about it was that it was somewhere between San Luis Pass in the Animas Mountains and the Alamo Huecos and was named after the Ho Che Min trail of Viet Cong fame. Since 81 ran between the two ranges, and since illegals needed to get to some sort of road to be picked up and hauled to sanctuary, Bernie was pretty sure she could find these pathways. In fact, Henry's remark had rankled, even though he was smiling at her when he said it. And it still rankled.

Her pager summoned. She extracted the phone and turned it on, wondering why she wasn't being contacted by the radio. She had an exciting, but momentary and illogical, thought that it might be Jim Chee calling. He'd had time to get the letter she'd sent him. But he wouldn't know her pager number. It would be some confidential stuff, maybe. Henry had warned her about dopers eavesdropping on their calls.

"Officer Manuelito," she said, still hoping.

"This is Ed Henry. Where are you?"

Bernie exhaled. "On I-10. Almost to Hatchita."

"Do a U across the divider and get on back here to the office. Some things I forgot to talk to you about."

"Oh?"

"About signs to spot. Evidence. What to take pictures of. Did you take any last week? If you did, bring 'em along. I need to see how you're doing."

Bringing along the pictures was no problem. The half of them she hadn't put in the envelope with the letter to Jim were still in the two-for-the-price-of-one Walgreen's photos sack, along with the roll of negatives. Not the sort of stuff you'd shoot for a contest, Bernie thought, as she flipped through them, but the oryx showed up well in the telephoto picture. Beautiful animal, she thought. Why would anyone consider killing one of them a sport?

Ed Henry gave the oryx hardly a glance. He spent more time studying, and criticizing, portraits on tire treads, broken-down thistles, snapped stems, footprints, and the like, and then went back to her pictures at the building site.

"Why did you go in there? No Trespassing sign and all?"

Bernie explained it. First thinking the truck she'd noticed would lead her back to the highway, then being curious about the Mexican license plate, and what it was doing out in that empty landscape. Being allowed entry, and finding that the truck was part of a watering place construction project.

Henry nodded, finding it sensible.

"I don't think I told you about the Tuttle Ranch," he said, looking up from the photos. "Probably not. It's sort of a private arrangement."

Bernie shook her head.

"Well, the deal is like this. The Tuttle people are sort of subrosa partners of ours. They keep their eye out for the illegals, mules, stuff we'd like to know. Those watering places they have for the game animals attract the Mexicans too. The Tuttle people watch for them and tip us off. Things like that. All quiet because there are some people in the smuggling trade who wouldn't like that. Might react. You know what I mean?"

All through this account, Henry's eyes had been studying her.

"React?"

Henry nodded. "Get mean. Cut fences. Shoot those expensive African animals. Maybe shoot a Tuttle cowboy."

"You mean the illegals?"

"I mean those smuggling contractors. The coyotes. Take their money, slip 'em over the border, and dump 'em off. And maybe bring in a few sacks of cocaine on the side."

Bernie nodded again. "Yeah, the man who let me in said they'd had some vandalism."

"The bottom line to all this is the Tuttle people help us and in return we don't bother them. Some of the high-society Mexican big shots like to come in for some big-game hunting. We don't bother them about visas. Anything like that. And we don't go barging in there to pick up illegals. Just let them know. They sort of arrest them for us and we go haul them into jail."

"I didn't know anything about any of this," Bernie said.

Henry smiled at her. "Well, now you do. My fault anyway. Should have done my job and filled you in on all these little side issues." He shuffled through the photographs and extracted a close-up Bernie had taken of a tire tread.

"Why'd you take this one?"

"It looked unusual."

"It is," Henry said. "It's what we used to call a 'recap.' You take a worn-out tire and salvage it by replacing the original tread with new rubber.

Sort of melting it on. Not done here anymore. Or not much. But they still do it some places in Mexico."

"It looks like it has a sort of a tread," Bernie said.

"They press that into the rubber when it's soft. And the point is we've been seeing this odd-looking tire mark for several years now. We intercept a drug shipment, or a busload of illegals, and there it is."

"But you've never caught the driver?"

"Nope. Had a witness or two who think they saw the pickup. An old blue Ford 150, they think it was. Say they see it somewhere near where the action was. Driving by, driving away, parked, or something. Driver supposed to be a skinny man. Oldish."

"So if I see the truck that's leaving these tracks, I stop him?"

"No. Call it in and keep it in sight. Could be dangerous," Henry said. "Or most likely, nothing at all. Just coincidence." Henry gathered the prints and the negative roll into a pile, opened his desk drawer, swept it in, and shut the drawer. He gave Bernie a challenging look.

"This all of them?"

"Some of them I dumped," Bernie said. "Out of focus, or the film fogged or something."

A moment of silence. Henry looked doubtful.

"But those would be on the negatives, wouldn't they?"

"Sure," Bernie said, wondering what this was about.

"Now I need one more picture," Henry said. He opened the drawer again, extracted a pocket-sized camera, and made sure it was loaded. "Need one of you."

And what was this about? Her expression must have asked that question.

"I'll send it out to the Tuttle people so they'll know you," Henry said. "So they'll know you're a legitimate Customs Service Agent."

That stung a little. "Don't I look like one. Uniform, badge, all that."

"You didn't mention the jewelry," Henry said. "You're out of uniform and now I have photographic evidence to prove it if I ever need to fire you. I mean wearing that little silver fellow on your lapel. Looks like you're going to a party or something. That stickpin's pretty but it's not allowed when you're on duty."

Bernie touched the stickpin—an inch-long but skinny replica of a Navajo **yei** her clan called Big Thunder. Her mother's brother had given it to her at her **kinaalda** ceremony when the family had gathered to celebrate her new womanhood. "He will look after you," Hostiin Yellow had told her. "Have him with you any time you need help."

"I didn't know about that regulation," Bernie said. "The pin's a family thing. I just wear it for luck."

"Just have your luck off duty then," Henry said.

11

"Let's go over this again," Captain Largo said. "As I understand it, you want me to send you down to the Mexican border for a couple of days or so, so you can get yourself involved in a U.S. Customs Service situation, because maybe it's connected to an FBI case in which you're not supposed to be involved anyway. Is that what you're asking?"

Captain Largo was leaning back in his swivel chair. He had let his bifocals slide down his nose and was staring at Chee over them (and over three or four stacks of paperwork). Waiting patiently for Chee to come up with a response.

"Well," Chee said. "It could be that . . ."

Largo waited again, pushed his glasses back into proper position, shifted in his chair.

"Why not just walk in here and say something like, ah, like, 'Captain, I've got a bunch of leave time coming and things are sort of quiet around here now, why don't I take a few days and go down south and see how Bernie Manuelito is doing.' Why not try that approach?"

Largo was grinning when he said it, but Chee didn't see the humor in it.

"Because I'm uneasy about the situation. We have this peculiar homicide up here. Looks professional. Big federal cover-up, and all that. And then we find out there's some sort of connection down where Officer Manuelito is working."

"It's Customs Officer Manuelito now," Captain Largo said. "We lost her. And whatever is going on down there, if anything at all, it's going to be a Customs case and not ours."

"Not unless it connects with our homicide up here," Chee said. "Not unless it gives us a way to—"

Captain Largo made a dismissive gesture. "A way to what? Solve an FBI felony case? Way to get Sergeant Chee back on the Bureau's Bad Boy list? Why don't you just call that young woman. Call her and give her a report on the situation on the telephone?"

"I did that," Chee said.

Largo sighed, shook his head. "Oh, hell with it," he said. "Give Officer Yazzie a rundown on anything pressing while you're gone. And don't drive one of our vehicles down there."

"Yes, sir."

"And tell Bernie we miss her," Largo said.

Four hours later, Jim Chee was driving through Nutt, New Mexico, on Highway 26, taking advantage of the shortcut that took one from Interstate 25 to Interstate 10 without the long dogleg to Las Cruces, taking advantage of that five-mile-over-the-speed-limit State Police usually allowed. He was in such a hurry that he barely noticed how the slanting light of the setting sun changed the colors of the Good Sight Mountains to his right, and lit the very tips of Massacre Peak to his left, and because he still hadn't figured out how to deal with Bernadette Manuelito. Actually, he had figured it out five or six different ways. None of them seemed satisfactory. And now with the little town of Nutt miles behind him he was almost to Deming. Customs Agent Manuelito had said she would meet him at the coffee shop attached to the Giant Station just off the intersection. He had rehearsed how he would greet her, what he would say, all that. And then he had modified his

plan because his memory of how she had
sounded when he called her from Shiprock had
changed a little. He'd been kidding himself
when he thought she sounded so friendly.

Actually it had been all very formal except
right at first. Bernie had said: "Would you believe I really miss you, Jim. Imagine! Missing
your boss." And he knew that polite pause between the 'Jim' and the 'Imagine' was there to
give him time to say: "Bernie, I miss you too."
He'd wasted it by trying to think of exactly the
right way to say it. Something to let Bernie know
that he woke up every morning thinking about
her, and how empty life seemed with her out of
it. And while he was trying to think of how to say
that, he said something like, "Ah," or "Well,"
and before he could get it together, Bernie was
talking again. She'd said: "But we drive better
vehicles down here, and this new boss is nice.
He has a mustache." And thus the call had
ended with none of the things said he wanted to
say and Chee feeling thoroughly stupid and
forlorn.

Chee spotted a new-model Ford 150 such as
Bernie had described among the rows of huge
eighteen-wheelers the coffee shop had lured off
Interstate 10. He left his older and dirtier

pickup near it, walked into the shop. It was crowded. Mostly men. Mostly truckers Chee guessed. Bernie was in a booth, her back to the door, listening to an older woman sitting opposite her. An Indian woman, but not a Navajo. Sort of resembled a Zuñi. Probably an O'odham. That tribe had its reservation on the Mexican border, lapping over into Arizona. The woman noticed him, smiled, said something to Bernie. Probably telling Bernie the Navajo cop had arrived. Then she was gathering her things together, and Bernie was sliding out of the booth, coming toward him, smiling.

Chee sucked in a deep breath. "Hello, Bernie."

"Hello, Jim," she said. "This is my friend, Customs Officer Eleanda Garza. She lets me share her house down in Rodeo and she's helping teach me to be a Customs agent."

Chee took his eyes off of Bernie, saw Customs Officer Garza was holding out her hand, saying, "How do you do."

Chee took it, said, "Pleased to meet you."

"Have to be going," Garza said. "I'll leave you the booth."

"You think we could find a quieter place?" Chee asked.

"I doubt it," Bernie said. "It's Friday night. Night for eating out in Deming. We'd probably have to wait an hour for a table."

They took the booth, with Chee trying not to show his disappointment. She ordered iced tea. He ordered coffee, wound too tight for food. Then he worked through the standard delivery of news about mutual friends and lapsed into silence.

"Your turn now," Chee said. "Anything new with you before we get into what I want to tell you about. Are you having any problems?"

She considered that a moment, smiled. "Well, to tell the truth, I managed to get lost and I never thought I could do that anywhere. But, you know, different landscape, different set of mountains, even worse roads than we were dealing with. In fact, that's how I got to that Tuttle Ranch." She laughed. "I was trying to follow the truck that was going there. Figured he was heading back to Interstate 10."

"That's the rich guy's place? The one who's raising exotic animals for his friends to hunt?"

Bernie nodded.

"Close to here? I want to see that some day."

Bernie extracted a paper napkin from its holder and a pen from her purse. "Here we are," she said, and sketched a map—a line going east representing I-10, an intersection identified with a state road number, another intersection with a county road number, and dotted lines for dirt roads. That done, she explained the landmarks. "Trouble is, when you get here"—she tapped the end of the last line with the pen point—"you come to a No Trespassing sign and a locked gate."

"And where's the watering station they were making?"

"About four miles in from the gate. You can't see because it's beyond a ridge. Anyway, they keep the gate locked. So first you have to persuade someone to let you in."

Chee picked up the map and studied it. Typical of Bernie, it was neatly done. He noticed Bernie was studying him, looking expectant. And looking beautiful, which made him even more nervous than he had been.

"You talk now," she said. "You said you wanted to tell me something."

Chee picked up his coffee cup, took a sip, cleared his throat. "Maybe we should get your supervisor in on that," he said. "Mr. Henry, isn't it?"

Bernie looked down at her hands for a moment, and then looked up at him. Expression strained. "Tell me first," she said.

"Well, I pretty well already have," Chee said.

"You just wanted to tell me about the name of the welding company being the same? That made you worry, I mean? Was there anything you didn't want to say on a telephone line?"

What did that mean, Chee wondered. He laughed, shook his head, looked embarrassed. "That and some odds and ends."

"You thought the line might be tapped?"

"I think that's unlikely," Chee said. "But then a few days ago I would have thought it highly unlikely that a fellow on the Jicarilla Reservation could find a credit card in a garbage can, use it to buy gas, and within three days somebody in Washington knows where he used the card."

Bernie's eyebrows raised. She said: "Did that happen?" And then: "Whose card was it?" But she didn't sound as if she cared.

"A fellow who seems not to have existed," Chee said. "At least the local FBI folks who're in charge of the case aren't saying."

Bernie held up her hand. "OK. Start at the beginning. But before you do, and before you decide whether you want Supervisor Henry in on all of this, would it help you to know that Henry grilled me about why I followed that welding truck out to the Tuttle Ranch. He said Customs, or anyway our local Customs crew, has a special deal with that ranch. And he had me give him all the photos. Like the ones I sent you. Even the negatives."

Early in this discourse, Chee had leaned forward, intent. Now he said: "Special deal?"

"He said Tuttle's watering holes for the animals attract dehydrated illegals," Bernie said. "So Tuttle's ranch hands watch for that and tip off Customs. In return, Customs doesn't go onto the ranch."

Chee was frowning. "Did Henry already know you'd taken the pictures? Or did you volunteer that?"

Bernie leaned back in the booth. Shook her head. "I should have thought of that," she said. "I really don't remember. I had brought them along to show him, but I sort of think he'd brought it up first."

"Did you notice anything especially interesting about the welding truck?"

She shook her head. "Nothing I saw. And the only pictures Mr. Henry remarked about were a shot of an oryx and one of a sort of worn-out tire track. A sort of recapped tire repair done in Mexico. He said it was like one on a truck they were watching for."

"Not the welding truck?"

"No. Then he asked me if this was all of my pictures, and I said except for a couple of negatives that didn't come out, and he put the pictures and the negatives back into the sack and into his desk drawer."

"Same sack the developer put them in?"

"Yes," Bernie said, and then paused and grimaced. "And now you're going to ask if it was one of those two-prints-for-the-price-of-one deals, and I'll say yes, and you'll say then Mr. Henry will know there's another set of those pictures somewhere."

"Yeah," Chee said. "But it probably doesn't matter."

"I hope not," Bernie said. "Except him wondering why I misled him." She was remembering the "TWO PRINTS—ONE PRICE" printed in big red letters on the sack she had given Henry.

"Anyway, I think we should have this conversation without inviting Mr. Henry into it unless we see some way he can help solve the puzzle."

Chee had lost his focus on the puzzle, let his

mind wander, thinking that Bernie was even more . . . More what? Beautiful than he'd remembered? Well, yes. But that wasn't it. Not exactly. In a Miss America contest, Janet Pete would have won. Representing perfection. Polish. Suavity. And if the pick was based purely on the sensual, then Mary Landon would wear the crown. He'd never forget the day he met her. Looking for a suspect at the Crownpoint rug auction where Mary was—as he finally realized—looking for the proper trophy to take back to Wisconsin to sire her Wisconsin children. And Janet, the half-Navajo vision of high-society sophistication, seeking the appropriate Navajo male willing to be taught the value system of urbane America. Ah, he missed them both. Either one would have been far better than this loneliness he was living through now. Who the hell was he to think he could find the perfect love? To think Bernie would settle for him. How many men found perfection? Well, there was Lieutenant Leaphorn and Emma, maybe. Did he think he could match the Legendary Leaphorn?

Chee noticed Bernie had stopped talking. Her face had flushed. She was staring at him. Just, he realized, as he'd been staring at her.

"Well?" Bernie said.

"I'm sorry," Chee said.

"Well, what do you think?"

A bunch of youngish people a table away had settled their division of their joint check and were noisily preparing to leave. "I was thinking of you, Bernie," Chee said. "I was thinking you're wonderful." But he said it well under the clamor of the departure.

Bernie gave the departees an irritated glance. "I'm sorry. I didn't understand that."

"I think I'd like to see if your boss knows how we can find Seamless Weld," Leaphorn said.

Bernie considered that. "But how do you do that without explaining why you're curious. Letting him know I sent you that picture?"

Chee had a sudden idea. "Maybe then he'd fire you," he said. "Then I could get you to come back and work for me."

He knew by the time he finished that it hadn't been a good idea. Bernie's face was flushed again.

"One of Sergeant Chee's officers?" she said, in a tone that was approximately neutral.

"I didn't mean that the way it sounded,"

Chee said. "I mean we'd be glad to have you back. Captain Largo said so too."

But the mood had changed now. Bernie said he must be worn out, hard drive and all. And she had a busy day herself tomorrow. Chee asked if they could get together tomorrow night. Now that they weren't wearing the same uniform, maybe they could have a dinner date. Anyway, he wanted to talk to her again. With that, Bernie drove away in her Ford 150, and Chee took his pickup back to the Motel 6, went to bed, and—feeling more like a damn fool, a cowardly damn fool—he tried to sleep.

12

Eleanda Garza's voice was cool and efficient.

"I'm sorry, Sergeant Chee," she said. "Bernie's not here."

"She's not? Ah, where can I—"

"If you called, she said to tell you she had to go to a meeting. For the new CPOs. A training session, I think it is."

"Oh. Ah, well, do you know when she will be back?"

He had tried to keep the disappointment out of his voice. Apparently he'd failed. Mrs. Garza's tone changed from cool to sympathetic. "I think this thing just came up suddenly. You know how it is when you work in law enforcement."

"Well, thank you, Mrs. Garza. It was good to meet you. Did Bernie leave a message?"

"I don't think she had time. I think she really wanted to talk to you."

"Thanks," Chee said.

"I'll tell her you called. And please try again. It's lonesome down here for Bernie."

Chee sat a moment looking at the telephone, feeling even more disgusted with himself, and with fate, than he had when he woke up. He paid his motel bill, put his stuff into his bag, the bag into his pickup, and began the drive northward from the very bottom of New Mexico toward its top—a long, lonely drive back to his empty trailer home under the cottonwood trees beside the San Juan at Shiprock. Empty and untidy and cramped and silent. At Lordsburg, he pulled into a service station, filled his tank, and sat awhile studying the map Bernie had sketched on her napkin. He would delay the depressing arrival at his trailer by finding the formal entrance to the Tuttle Ranch. He'd use another couple of hours finding the place on the other side of that huge spread where Bernie had caught up with the Seamless Weld truck.

Finding the front entrance of the Tuttle Ranch was simple enough. The elderly lady at the Giant Station cash register explained it.

"Get off Interstate 10 at Gage, take County

Road 2, and then 20 toward JBP Mountain and—"

"Hold it," Chee said. "Show me on my map."

The cashier frowned, looked at the map, put her pencil tip on a hump labeled "JBP Mountain" and traced it along. "Then past Soldiers Farewell Hill, right here, and take the turn south toward the Cedar Mountains"—she tapped with her pencil point—"and then you pass Hattop Mountain"—another pencil tap— "and turn right on a dirt road there. It's graded but they never put any gravel on it. You'll see a big corner post at the junction pointing southward and a sign on it says 'Tuttle Ranch.' But if you're looking for Tuttle, he's not there much. Lives somewhere back east."

The sign nailed to the corner post was painted in neat red block letters: TUTTLE RANCH—SEVEN MILES. The legend neatly painted below read: PRIVATE PROPERTY. ENTRY BY PERMISSION ONLY.

Chee paused here a moment, comparing the landmarks Bernie had indicated on her napkin to the large-scale Benchmark map he kept in his truck. After about ninety minutes, several wrong turns, and much dust, he found the road along which Bernie had followed the Seamless Weld truck, and the ridge she had mentioned crossing just before she had reached the locked gate and encountered Tom O'day. He stopped on the ridge, got out his binoculars, and checked. He saw the gate, but no one was there to open it for him even if he could show them a reason they should. He scanned the landscape. Mountain ridges in every direction, but dry mountains here. Far to the east the Floridas and to the west, the Big and Little Hatchets. Far beyond them and blue with distance, the ragged shapes of the Animas and Peloncillos. Chee was comfortable with the emptiness of his tribe's Four Corners country, but here all he could see seemed to be a lifeless total vacuum.

But not quite lifeless. Across the fence and far down the ridge away from the locked gate his eye caught motion. He refocused the binoculars. Five great gray beasts, two with long curved horns, were walking in a line down a slope. But going where?

Apparently into a playa where runoff water would collect if rain ever fell here. In the playa a windmill stood beside a circle of what seemed to be a water tank.

The sound of an engine. Chee shifted his

binoculars toward it. A truck towing a horse trailer was rolling down the hill toward the gate.

Chee climbed into his own pickup and headed for the gate. The driver of the ranch truck was standing behind it now, looking about thirty years younger than the man Bernie had described. About seventeen maybe, grinning, with his hat pushed to the back of his head.

"'Fraid you hit a dead end here," he said. "I can't let you through."

"I saw your sign," Chee said. "But maybe you can help me out with some information."

"If I can. Where you from?"

"Up in San Juan County. Navajo Reservation."

"I saw you was Indian," the boy said. "But down here we got a lot of Indians, but mostly the local tribe and some Apaches. Got three of them on our team."

Chee studied the boy. "Football, I'd say. You a tight end, or maybe fullback."

The boy laughed. "Little school there at Gage. We played six man. We didn't have all those positions."

"If you could unlock that gate for me, I'd go down that road just far enough to take a look at that new watering tank you're putting in."

"Watering tank down the road? I don't know nothing about that. The only water tank out that direction is way over yonder." He pointed in the direction of the playa where Chee had seen the windmill. "In the spring, and again after the rainy season, water drains down into that low place, and soaks in. They put a little windmill there to pump it into the drinking tank when the playa goes dry."

"Well, I don't know," Chee said. "But a man at the Chevron station at Lordsburg told me about it. He's a rancher around here somewhere, and I was telling him about the trouble we were having keeping our stock watered, and how I was looking for some used tanks we could buy. Anyway, he said the Tuttle Ranch was putting in some new tanks for those African animals you're raising and was selling off their old metal tanks."

The boy shrugged. "News to me."

"This fella said it involved some sort of new construction a few miles inside the Southeast Gate. Would this be the Southeast Gate?"

"Hey," the boy said. "I bet I know what he was talking about." He pointed. "They're putting in some sort of a structure over the hill there." He pointed. "Just three or four miles beyond that hill. There was a crew in there doing some digging and pouring concrete. They put up a house of some sort and mounted a little windmill on it, but I think it was just to run an electric generator, and the building was to store stuff in. I don't think it had anything to do with water. And then just yesterday I was by there and the sparks were flying. They were doing some metal cutting and welding. Working on pipes, it looked like. Nothing like a water tank."

Chee considered that. "Well, the man at the Chevron said they were installing a windmill to pump water for the animals."

The boy was grinning. "I heard that too. But it's to run a little electric generator. To get to the water table here, you'd have to drill down damn near like an oil well. Hundreds of feet. Probably thousands. Take's a big rig to do that. Nothing like that's been in here."

"I'd sure like to see what they've done," Chee said. "How about it? No harm done."

"They don't give me the key."

"Why don't I just climb over the fence and walk over there. Not more than three or four miles you said?"

The boy took off his hat, studied Chee thoughtfully, rubbed his tangled blond hair, and restored the hat.

"No, sir. I'd just have to get out my cell phone here and report it. And somebody would come out and run you off. And maybe I'd get fired."

So Chee said thanks, anyway. He drove back up the hill he'd come in on and found what he was looking for—fading tracks leading off from the road in the proper direction. They would have been made hauling in post hole diggers, posts, spools of wire, and all else needed when that formidable fence was built. Chee jolted down the tracks to the fence, and along it, around the slope of the hill, and up the next one. Near the top of it he stopped. The gate where he met the boy was out of sight now, but in the valley below he could see down where a little building stood with a small windmill mounted on its roof.

He got out his binoculars again and studied it. The boy was right. The blades were connected on the platform to a drive shaft that terminated in what was probably a gearbox. That was mounted atop what looked like the housing for a generator. Chee could also make out insulated cables running down one of the walls of the shack and disappearing into it. It was not an unusual sight for Chee. Many family outfits around the reservations established such electrical sources for their hogans to run refrigerators and their television sets. But what would it be used for here? Hard to tell from what was visible to him. But he could make out the edge of what appeared to be a fairly large excavation. There were pipes in that.

Back on the access road, he headed for Interstate 10 and then turned north toward Shiprock. It had been a long, long day of driving and a total, absolute waste of time. Almost anyway. He had learned that Bernie was getting along a lot better without him than he was without her. And he had added another vague little bit of information to be considered in a vague murder case, which was none of his business anyway. Officially not his affair.

But Bernie was his affair. At least he wanted her to be. And Bernie's boss seemed to have a peculiar interest in this welding truck and in what Bernie saw beyond the Tuttle Ranch gate. He was feeling increasingly uneasy about that. He was suspecting what Bernie had photographed had nothing to do with anything as innocent as watering exotic animals.

13

Former Lieutenant Joe Leaphorn was making a hurried effort to tidy up his living room. Someone named Mary Goddard was coming over to interview him. Not a visit he expected. He knew almost nothing about this woman except she worked for **U.S. News and World Report,** formerly with the **Baltimore Sun,** and that she wanted to ask him about that peculiar homicide up on the border of the Jicarilla Reservation.

"Why me?" Leaphorn had asked. "Didn't you tell her I'm just a civilian. That it's an FBI case anyway, and—"

Georgia Billie was the senior secretary in the NTP administration office, but she had never quite come to think of Lieutenant Leaphorn as legendary.

"Joe. Joe," she said. "Of course I did. I told her you'd gotten old and grumpy and didn't like to be bothered and you wouldn't know anything about it anyway but she just grinned at me and said you were still the Legendary Lieutenant and she'd like to meet you anyway."

That produced a moment of silence.

"You didn't give her my number did you? Or my address?"

"She already had your address."

Leaphorn sighed. Said: "Oh, well."

"In fact, she's on her way out there now. Instead of acting like you're mad at me, you should be thanking me for the warning." She laughed. "I'm giving you some time to sneak out the back door and hide."

But he didn't. His curiosity had kicked in. What was it about this homicide that had brought a reporter from the best of the national newsmagazines all the way to Window Rock? Maybe she knew something that would cast some light on this affair.

The Mary Goddard who introduced herself at his door did not resemble the smooth-faced, glossy women reporters television had taught Leaphorn to expect. She was short, sturdy, and obviously middle-aged. The heavy layers of makeup with which white women so often coated their faces were missing. Her smile, which looked to Leaphorn warm and friendly, revealed natural-looking teeth and not the chalk-white caps displayed by TV celebrities.

"I'm Mary Goddard," she said, handing him a business card. "I'm a reporter, and I came here hoping you'll have time to talk to me."

"Come on in," Leaphorn said, and pointed her to a chair. "If you like coffee, I have a pot brewed in the kitchen."

"Please," Ms. Goddard said. "Black."

He remembered to put the cups on saucers as Emma would have done had she not left him a widower, or Professor Bourbonette would have had she not been up on the Southern Ute Reservation collecting oral history tales. He also brought in napkins and then seated himself across the coffee table from Goddard.

She sipped, made an approving face. Leaphorn sipped, trying to decide what Goddard's first question would be. It would concern what progress was being made on the homicide investigation, and his answer would be that the FBI was handling it and he didn't know anything about it.

She restored her cup to its saucer.

"Mr. Leaphorn," she began, "I wonder how you managed to get an official of the Bank of America to ask questions in the bank's credit card administration about a credit card issued to Carl Mankin. Could you tell me that?"

Far from what he'd expected. He looked at Ms. Goddard with sharply increased interest. He was dealing with a professional here.

"Did that happen?"

"It did," she said. And waited.

Leaphorn chuckled, already enjoying this. "My turn now. How do you know? And what brought you to me?"

"You're retired, aren't you. Technically not involved in any way in any of this. But a sergeant who used to be your assistant had jurisdiction, or did, more or less, until the FBI took over. Is that right?"

"Right."

"As I understand from my sources in Washington, this sergeant—Jim Chee, isn't it?—he had someone in his local bank make inquiries about a Visa card held by someone killed in San Juan County, New Mexico. The inquiry ran into an FBI stop order and that ended that." She combined a hand gesture with a change of expression to signify finality. Then smiled at Leaphorn and said: "However!"

Leaphorn smiled.

"However, not much later the same inquiry comes in from the important direction—from the top instead of the bottom. It hits the same federal roadblock. But this time the bank's big shots are involved. The kind of folks not used to being told no by the FBI or anyone else. This gets chatted about at their two-martini lunches. One of the power brokers asks his lobby lawyer. People talk to a senator whose campaign they helped finance. Somebody calls the chairman of the subcommittee that oversees the Department of the Interior, and so it goes. About then I ask myself, What's making this credit card such a big deal? Why are these busy moguls getting so interested in this homicide way out in San Juan County, New Mexico?"

Goddard picked up her cup, looked over the rim at Leaphorn, took another sip.

"That's the same question I'm asking," Leaphorn said. He looked at her business card. "**U.S. News and World Report**. Not the sort of publication that goes after sin, sex, and sensation. And it wouldn't care much about a murder

out here. Not unless it was somehow signifi-
cant."

Goddard clicked her cup back into the
saucer.

"Murder, was it?"

"Well, now," Leaphorn said. "I believe the
last news account I've seen said the FBI reported it still under investigation. But the talk
I've heard over my enchilada down at the
Navajo Inn is about a stranger being shot in the
back. Hard to call a back shot a suicide."

Goddard nodded. "Yes. Even in Washington.
But there they might rule it an accident."

Leaphorn chuckled. "If the press gets after
the U.S. District Attorney, I suspect that will be
suggested." He shrugged. "It might be true. But
then he'd have to explain some—" He stopped,
sipped his coffee, gestured toward her cup.

"No thanks," she said. "But go on. Explain
what? I don't really know anything about the
crime itself."

"Should we exchange information?" Leaphorn asked. "If we do I need to make some
rules. I want you in a position to tell a grand jury
you promised your source confidentiality. That
way, I don't get called and have to protect my

sources by being held in contempt and locked away for a while."

"And who are your sources?"

"Are we off the record?"

"How about I call you a source close to the Navajo Tribal Police?"

"How about I'm someone knowledgeable about law enforcement in the Four Corners?"

She nodded. "Deal," she said. "Minor change in the syntax, but nothing that would single you out. Now tell me why it's murder and not an accident."

"Body stripped of all identification," Leaphorn said. "Nothing in pockets except small change and keys to a rental car. Car found miles from the body. Too far to walk."

"Murder," she said, nodding. "Wallet gone, which brings us to the Visa card."

"Found by a trash collector cleaning up a park on the Jicarilla Navajo Reservation. The card was used at one of those pay-outside filling stations, and tracked to one of the trash collector's in-laws. And now we get to my question, still unanswered. What brought you out here?"

"Fair enough," she said. "Now you have to understand that we'll be talking about

Washington. The big shots are trading information about what could be going on out in Indian country. What is causing someone with the clout to get it done to want to cause the FBI to cover up a shooting like this one. With the victim nobody in particular, and the crime done nowhere in particular. Doing that takes big political muscle. But who's using that muscle? And why? So I start thinking there could be a big story there."

She stopped, peered at Leaphorn. "Does that answer your question?"

Leaphorn considered. "Part of it, I guess."

"Well then," said Goddard, "I will add that I was already interested because a woman who works in the Security and Exchange Commission has become very, very frustrated because she can't find out"—Goddard paused again and smiled at Leaphorn—"not to her satisfaction anyway, can't find out how her husband got killed in San Juan County, New Mexico."

She waited for a reaction from Leaphorn.

"How about some more coffee," he said, provoking only a negative gesture that, in turn, provoked him to violate one of his rules and show off a little.

"I understand the FBI has not been very

forthcoming in this case," he said. "What were they telling Mrs. Mankin?" Having asked that, having demonstrated that he already knew the victim's name, having strutted a bit for this woman, he watched carefully for her reaction. Once again, she surprised him.

"Mrs. Who?" she asked, looking genuinely puzzled. "I don't know about her."

"The widow," Leaphorn said, slightly flustered. "Mrs. Carl Mankin."

"Do you mean the victim's widow? The victim's widow is Mrs. Ellen Stein. Or more formally, Mrs. Gordon Stein."

Leaphorn leaned back in his chair, considering this bombshell, deciding he'd get back to it later and in the future would suppress the temptation to show off.

"But you still haven't told me why the death of this man, this Mr. Gordon Stein, interests your magazine."

"It doesn't," Goddard said. "Not unless it connects in some way with what happened to about forty billion dollars that seems to have disappeared from the Indian Trust Fund. A sort of evaporation that the General Accounting Office thinks has been going on since way back when."

Leaphorn leaned forward again, said: "Forty billion. I read about that in that suit the lawyer, Covell, wasn't it, filed against the Secretary of the Interior. I thought maybe that number was a typographical error. Too many zeros on the end of the number. And you think this homicide of ours might be connected?"

"Maybe. At least indirectly."

"Like how?"

"Look," Goddard said. "I cover politics, not crime. Although I admit sometimes they're connected and hard to tell apart. The homicide interests me because this Covell lawsuit could pry the lid off the biggest federal corruption case since President Harding's great Teapot Dome Scandal. You probably already know this, but I'll remind you. The General Accounting Office has already established that the Department of the Interior has failed to collect, lost, or let somebody steal billions from the royalties supposed to go into the tribal trust funds. The federal district court has already held both the Secretary of the Interior and the Secretary of the Treasury in contempt of court for allowing records of trust money to be destroyed. Fined them six hundred thousand dollars, but that's being appealed."

Leaphorn chuckled. "I've heard about all that. The Secretary of the Interior got a lot of attention out here when she shut down the department's computer system for overhaul. A lot of tribal members went three months without their royalty checks."

"And were protesting loudly to their congressmen. Especially the delegations from here, and Arizona, Utah, Oklahoma, and Texas, to name a few. And that is getting us to the story that really interests me."

Goddard waited for Leaphorn to say: "What's that?" But he had reverted to his traditional Navajo habit of just waiting for the speaker to speak.

"That story if I can dig it out is politics," Goddard said. "Huge amounts of blame to be spread here. In politics blame is just as useful as praise. Senators can be defeated, contenders can be elected, resulting power shifts in committees, so forth." She extracted a notebook from her purse, flipped pages. "Oil," she said. "Osage, Seminole, and Choctaw fields, etcetera, in Oklahoma, out here the Bisti and Windmill fields and others, and big ones on Indian land in Wyoming, Kansas, elsewhere. Navajo coal, Hopi coal, Zuñi coal. Timber, copper, silver, so forth, from the northern tribes. You Navajos and the Jicarilla Apaches are probably the biggest losers in terms of natural gas, but remember those Four Corners open pit coal mines. And speaking of this territory, that area where Stein was killed, that San Juan Basin field has more than twenty thousand producing wells—mostly methane and natural gas. It's the world's largest source of gas."

"I'm going to pour us each a fresh cup of coffee," Leaphorn said. "Then I want to talk about why our Carl Mankin is your Gordon Stein."

With the coffee poured, Leaphorn told Goddard what he knew about the Carl Mankin Visa card, how it had been recovered and how quickly control of the case had shifted from Farmington to Washington. Goddard provided the time Stein's body had been delivered to a Washington funeral home—five days after Cowboy Dashee had photographed it.

"And by the way," she added, "Mrs. Stein got an unofficial and confidential report from someone high in the FBI that an intensive hunt was on for several local Apaches believed to have been hunting deer in the area on the day of the shooting."

Leaphorn laughed. "Out of season of

course," he said. "Deer poachers. Ideal suspects when you need suspects. So I guess the top folks in the FBI intend to put it in the books as another hunting accident with the culprits fleeing the scene to avoid a game-law violation rap." He shook his head. "But Miss Goddard, I want you to know this isn't the way the local agents operate. Some of them are pretty green at normal criminal work, but what you're dealing with in this case is beyond their control. Don't give them the blame. It's Washington."

She nodded. "I can add that Stein had both a B.S. and an M.S. in Petroleum Engineering from the University of Oklahoma. He'd worked for Welltab, and briefly for El Paso Natural, and for the Williams Company, one of the really big ones in pipelining everything, from oil to everything else."

She sipped her coffee again. Studied Leaphorn. Sighed. "I think I will go ahead and tell you something I'm not supposed to know because I was told it in confidence by someone who wasn't supposed to know it either."

"So I have to promise it stops with me," Leaphorn said.

Goddard nodded.

"OK, I promise."

"Stein also worked a lot in the Middle East. In Yemen, for example, and in Saudi Arabia and Iraq. Oil field and pipeline stuff, officially," Goddard said. "But most likely with the Central Intelligence Agency paying a share of his expenses and getting its share of what he was learning."

Leaphorn sat with his hands folded on his stomach, intertwining the fingers, making roofs of them, making fists, while he thought. "To sum it up, would it be fair to say you think Stein might have been sent out here to see how this great network of pipelines we have all around us might have been used to siphon off some of that forty billion bucks?"

"Who knows? But wouldn't that make a wonderful story?"

"And also fair to say that Stein might also still be doing some CIA work? What's the CIA interest?"

"Maybe some sort of money-laundering scheme. You know, the theory is that Saudi oil money is sponsoring the Al Qaeda terrorist operation. Don't ask me to guess at that connection. Swapping oil, maybe, so the money can't be traced?"

Leaphorn nodded. "And if Stein was out hunting the way oil and gas was pipelined out to folks not paying for it, maybe that hunter wasn't careless," Leaphorn said.

"Maybe he was hunting Stein," Goddard said. "Maybe it was Osama bin Laden or one of his terrorists. An even better story."

"You think Stein was working for the CIA? As I used to understand the law, the Agency is supposed to leave the inside the U.S.A. stuff to the FBI. Not that those security people paid much attention to that sort of red tape."

"I guess it's possible," Goddard said. "But I think it's more likely the motivation was politics. Maybe the Department of Justice, maybe Interior, or one of its divisions. Or more likely one of the big-money operatives in either the Republican or Democratic Party, hunting for campaign ammunition, or one of the environmental protection outfits with a different ax to grind. Maybe even the Libertarian Party wanting to prove how hopelessly inept the federal government is these days."

"Another question," Leaphorn said. "Who wanted Stein shot?"

Goddard grinned at him. "Let me know if you find out." The grin faded away. "And if you do find out, remember it has to be someone with connections powerful enough to force the FBI brass to cover it up."

14

Customs Patrol Officer Bernie Manuelito was no longer feeling like an utter novice in this business of guarding the Republic's boundary line. She had learned the language of her new profession, taken part in two "nettings" of illegals, and had personally detected a "mule track" down which "carpet people" had been carrying loads of illegal skag, coke, and refined pot. She understood the difference between mere illegal immigrants and mules who were also illegals but were hired to haul bales of controlled substances in on their backs—sort of like FedEx deliveries. Near the dangerous top of all this were the "coyotes" and the buyers. The coyotes were the travel agents and tour guides of those who came to cross the border into the land of milk and honey, promising to get them safely past Bernie and her fellow CPOs to some community where the phony credentials the coyotes sold them would qualify them for minimum-wage jobs. The receivers, of course, were those who met the mules and warehoused the cocaine, heroin, and pot until it could be delivered to dealers who, in turn, delivered it to their customers in country clubs, corporate boardrooms, honky-tonk bars, chic nightclubs, sorority and frat houses, and bar-association meetings where those who could afford the stuff bought it and used it.

Bernie's dream was to nab a receiver and follow him all the way back to the high-rise, glass-walled, deep-carpeted office of the banker who financed the operation and haul them both to jail in the banker's limo. But that wouldn't happen soon. From what she had seen as a cop, the so-called War on Drugs filled the jails with addicts and the nickel-and-dime peddlers, but left the drug czars unmolested. And from what she was seeing now, as a Customs patrol officer, she wouldn't change that soon. If she made an arrest today it would be a little family of destitute Mexicans.

She was standing on one of the numerous

ridges of Big Hatchet Mountain looking south-ward into the gap between her ridge and an ad-joining volcanic outcrop identified on her map as Bar Ridge. She saw an old-model school bus converted into a sort of van—its windows cov-ered with plywood and its top loaded with bun-dles, boxes, and rolls of bed clothing and two mattresses.

A man in stained coveralls was squatting be-side the bus doing something to the front wheel. Nearby, sitting, standing, or prone, she could count five others taking cover from the sun in the sparse shade of the mesquite brush growing beside the outcrop.

Bernie reached into the cab of her pickup, got the mike, pushed the proper buttons. "Manuelito again," she said. "I count five people now. Man trying to fix the bus. Another man, a woman, toddler-sized boy, and a girl, maybe six or seven."

"That global positioning you gave me put you at Big Hatchet Mountain," the dispatcher said. "That look right?"

"It does to me. But not much of a mountain to be called big."

"Smaller down here, but rougher. The nearest backup I could find for you is a unit south of Road Forks and he's tied up for a while. If you think they're running dope I could send down a chopper from Tucson. What do you think?"

"I think we're looking at a family of starved-out farmers. I think they got off on the wrong track and ruined their front suspension."

"OK, then. Keep an eye on 'em. Let me know if they're moving out, or if anyone shows up to haul them away." He paused. "And remember, Miss Manuelito, they're illegals. That's criminals. C-R-I-M-I-N-A-L-S. Don't do anything dumb."

Whereupon, after a few more minutes of watching the driver struggling with the front wheel, after remembering the painful plight of the half-starved and dehydrated illegals she had helped round up a week earlier, Bernie decided she'd rather do something dumb than be ashamed of herself. It was standard practice for Customs officers patrolling in desert country to carry oversized canteens. Since a painful arrest of last week in which the illegals had been almost dead of dehydration, Bernie had also been taking along two big plastic jugs of water just in case.

She drove down the ridge, circled carefully through the brush and cactus, and found the still-fresh tracks the bus must have left. She followed them around the corner of the Big Hatchet toward the Bar Ridge outcrop. The bus was there, but no humans were in sight. Bernie wasn't surprised. They would have heard her coming, seen the Customs vehicle, and would be hiding somewhere.

She parked behind the bus, got her pistol out of the glove box, and put on her holster, took the battery megaphone from its rack, and stepped out of her pickup.

"Amigos," she shouted. **"Tengo agua para ustedes."** She listened, heard no response, and repeated the call, with one small revision in her classroom-and-border Spanish, changing **amigos** to **amiga,** to appeal to the woman she'd seen. "I'm Border Patrol," she shouted, "but you have nothing to fear from me. I will give you water. I will help you." Then she put the megaphone on the truck roof, studied the brushy ridge, listened, and heard nothing.

Bernie dropped the truck's tailgate, extracted her water jugs, and put them on the hood. **"Agua para usted. Por la niña y el niño."**

Again, no answer. What now?

A man was hurrying through the brush

toward her, waving. She had the sudden thought that perhaps she had been stupid and felt for the snap on her holster flap. Then she saw the man seemed to be crying. Or was he laughing? Whatever, he didn't seem threatening. And he was babbling something in Spanish. It was, "Thank God you found us."

Bernie raised her hand. "Hold it," she said. "Do you speak English? Who are you?"

"I was coming to get these people," he said in fluent English. He pointed to the bus. "But it broke. Going over a rock."

"You can't fix it?" Bernie asked. "And who are you?"

The young man in the greasy coveralls straightened, drew a deep breath. "My name is Delos Vasquez. I am a mechanic." Then he gestured toward the jugs. "Water, you said. I must call Mr. Gomez and his family."

"Sure," Bernie said, thinking the man looked totally harmless. Not much taller than her and skinny. About thirty, with large, brown, sad-looking eyes. Now she noticed Mr. Gomez and his family emerging from the hillside brush and moving cautiously toward them. Gomez wore a straw hat, a neatly trimmed white beard, and was carrying the little girl.

Vasquez motioned, shouted in Spanish. Something about water but Bernie didn't catch much of it. She was in the truck cab, screwing the cap off her Thermos, handing that and the cup under it to Vasquez, motioning to him to help himself to the water.

He smiled at her. "No. The rule is that the women and children must go first."

While the woman and the children were dealing with their thirst, Vasquez brought over the bearded man. "May I present the father of my sister-in-law, Señor Miguel Gomez," he said. Señor Gomez bowed. So did Bernie, trying to remember the formal language of introduction. Failing that, she said: "Welcome to the United States."

"And this is Señora Catherina Vasquez, the **esposa** of my brother, and their children."

Catherina Vasquez, dusty, disheveled, looking utterly exhausted, managed a shy smile. So did the children.

My criminals, Bernie thought.

Before the Border Patrol shuttle arrived Bernie had improved her Spanish a little and collected from Vasquez and Mr. Gomez an account of how he and the Gomez group happened to be here. Gomez, so the story went, had gone to San Pedro Corralitos to get work at the copper smelter there because there was no work at Nuevo Casas Grandes, where his family lived. But the smelter was still shut down, and the only work there was a crew repairing the pipeline that had brought the fuel in to fire its furnaces. So Mr. Gomez had paid a tour guide in Sabinas Hidalgo to bring his daughter, Catherina, and her children to visit Vasquez's mother in Lordsburg, so she could see her grandchildren. The coyote had taken them to the port of entry at Antelope Wells and given them visa credentials. Mr. Gomez showed these to Bernie, who recognized them instantly as examples of the fraudulent documents she'd been shown in training classes. With some translating help from Vasquez, Gomez told her the coyote had then taken them to the border fence, showed them where to cross it, and showed them where to wait until a truck would arrive to take them to Lordsburg. The truck arrived, took them up the road toward Interstate 10. But near this mountain he stopped, told Mr. Gomez a border patrol helicopter had flown over and seen them and they must get out and hide. He would come back and get them.

Here Vasquez took over. "I got a call in

Lordsburg yesterday. The son of a bitch told me where he had left them. He said he had to drop them off or everyone would have been arrested. So I came where he told me, and finally I found them." He shook his head, eyes sad. "If I hadn't they would have died."

That was the story Bernie was passing along to the dispatcher.

"Haven't got time for all this. But you can't believe it anyway."

"What he told me sounds logical enough. But I'm new in this business."

"No sign of coke. So forth?"

"Nothing easily visible. But I didn't pry into the luggage, or the tires or anything like that. They had hours to hide it. Does that Delos Vasquez name mean anything to you?"

"Vasquez around here is like Kelly in Boston or Jones in Texas or Begay at Window Rock," he said. "But Delos, that's unusual. Rings a bell. I think he showed up on a list of underlings of some big dealer at Agua Prieta. Down in Sonora."

"Do we have a warrant for him?"

"Just some gossip. Collect lots of that. Agua P's just over the border from Douglas. Good place for eavesdropping."

The Border Patrol van arrived, manned by two CPOs she'd never met. They introduced themselves as Billy and Lorenzo, and hand-cuffed Vasquez. Gomez, Catherina, and the children were shoed into the van and the door locked.

"We're going to search your bus," one of the backup crew said, "and we want you to stay right here with Officer Manuelito while we're doing that. If we have any questions we'll be calling you down."

Vasquez nodded.

They stood by the van, watching the bus being searched.

"They will be deported back to Mexico now," Vasquez said. "All their money gone to the damned coyote. Poorer than ever."

"How about you?"

"I'm a U.S. citizen," Vasquez said. "Probably I will have to spend some time in jail. But I don't know what they will charge me with."

"Maybe conspiring to violate the immigration law?"

"Yes. I guess I did that." He looked at her, expression sad. "But with family needing help, then you do what you have to do. And it wasn't anything about drugs. I wouldn't do that. Those men are evil."

"If I were you, or if I was your lawyer, I would give you some advice, Mr. Vasquez. When the federal authorities ask you about your part in this, I would start at the point where you get a call from the man who told you he had dropped off the family and they wanted you to pick them up and if you didn't you were afraid they would die of thirst. I would leave off all that first part. Let Mr. Gomez tell them about that."

Vasquez considered that. Nodded.

"Do you know those drug dealers in Mexico?"

"Two or three," he said. "At Agua Prieta, I was a driver for them for a while. But I didn't want to do that work. I didn't want to be around them."

Bernie nodded.

"I think you think I am a drug man," Vasquez said, shaking his head. "Or Mr. Gomez is one. But no."

During all this conversation, Vasquez had been studying her, and the little silver and turquoise replica of Big Thunder she was wearing on her collar.

"That is very pretty," he said, pointing to it. "That little silver stick man."

"He represents one of the Navajo spirits. My mother's brother made him for me. For luck. We call him Big Thunder." But Bernie didn't want this conversation to be so personal. She said: "Why didn't you want to be around them?"

"Well," he began, and stopped. "They kill people."

"I've heard that," she said.

He was frowning at her, looking hesitant and thoughtful.

"You have been very kind to us," he said. "Did you know they have your picture in Agua Prieta? Those men, I mean. I think the coyotes down there might be afraid of you."

"My picture?" Bernie said, startled. "I don't think so. How could they?"

"It was you," Vasquez said. "I noticed it the first time I saw you. Just like the picture they were showing around."

Bernie produced a shaky smile. "A lot of women look like me."

"This one was wearing that little silver stick man on her shirt. I noticed it in the photograph."

"But why would they have my picture? I don't understand that."

The men searching the bus shouted, motioning for Vasquez.

"Because they seemed to be afraid of you. So when any of them see you they will recognize you as a spy. And these people, when they are afraid of somebody, they want to kill them."

15

Winsor's houseman, George, brought the package into his living suite. It was one of those tough document-sized Airborne Express envelopes, originally delivered to his office and then relayed to his town house by messenger. It was marked "PERSONAL," and it came from El Paso, Winsor noticed, with the return address of the office of the lawyer he used there. He zipped it open and removed the contents.

Seven 8-by-12-inch black-and-white photographs and a note folded with them:

The answer to your Who question: Carl Mankin. No personal data available to us here.

The answer to your Why ques-

tion: Remember your order required extreme action.

Enclosed: the requested photos and photo of the CPO Officer who took them. Officer Bernadette Manuelito. Former Navajo Tribal Police Officer, transferred down from the Shiprock NTP district earlier this year with strong endorsement from NTP headquarters. Her photo taken by West.

Winsor looked at the photo of Bernie long enough to decide the woman, rewarding him with an embarrassed smile, was one of those who would never be called "cute." Pretty, yes. Probably a very handsome woman. More important for his interests, she looked intelligent. Noticeably intelligent. Smart. Clever. That led him to the photographs she had taken.

He set two aside with a glance, then focused on the Mexican standing beside a tool trailer glowering at the camera. He fished his magnifying glass from a desk drawer for a closer look. The tools he could identify were what one would expect in a mechanic's truck—assorted wrenches, measuring devices, pressure gauges, two fuel tanks. Probably propane or methane. Some were strange to him. But would they be strange to pipeline workers? Probably not.

Then he focused on a photo, obviously taken from a location above the work scene with a telescopic lens. It showed three big ugly animals walking along a hillside. Oryx, and one with a great curving, trophy-sized horn. Some of old man Tuttle's exotic game. The other photo looked directly down on the trucks, the men working around the excavation—and into the excavation. He picked up the magnifying glass again. Looked through it at the print, held his breath for a long moment, and then exhaled and produced an angry expletive.

He picked up his telephone, punched his houseman's number. While he waited he studied the photo of Bernie again. Why had she taken that photograph? Because she'd been sent there specifically to take it? Because something she'd seen had made her suspicious?

George's voice said: "Yes, sir."

"Get Budge," Winsor said. "Tell him to call me. Tell him it's urgent. Tell him to get the plane set for El Paso and then into Mexico. Then get me packed for four or five days. With walking shoes."

"Yes, sir," the houseman said.

Winsor sat back in his chair, shook his head, and muttered: "One damned thing after another." He picked up his "CONGRESS" file, opened it, and reread the fax Haret had sent him. The congressman from Oregon causing trouble as usual, their bought-and-paid-for Midwestern congressman forgetting why Winsor had financed his campaign and saying nothing helpful, and the marijuana bill undefeated, merely tabled for further consideration. A bad time to be leaving Washington.

A flash of reflected sunlight caught his attention. It came from the glass eye of the Bengal tiger head in the trophy room. He shut the folder, picked up the photographs from New Mexico, and looked at the little procession of oryx Officer Manuelito had photographed. Scimitar-horned oryx, he remembered, and the horns they carried justified the name. He'd take a rifle along. If he had time to shoot that big one, he'd use it to replace the head of the lion he'd shot in Kenya. It wasn't a very impressive lion and the trip hadn't been one that produced any happy memories.

He didn't expect any happiness out of this one, either. But he had to make it, to quit counting on others to get a job done. He'd handle it himself, with Budge there to lend a hand if needed. No way to guess what he'd find at the Tuttle Ranch. But if things were going bad there, or at the Mexican end of that project, he'd have to fix them. Otherwise it wouldn't matter much what happened in that congressional committee. Or at the bank.

16

Even before responding to Bernie's "welcome home," even while putting her overnight bag in the entry closet, Eleanda Garza was giving Bernie curious looks. Then she followed Bernie into the kitchen.

"Hey," she said. "I heard you made a bust of illegals. All by yourself. And I heard you sort of bent the rules some by taking risks. Is that right?"

Bernie was not in the mood this morning for any sort of criticism. "Risks?" she said. "A mother, two kids, and an old man. And a brother-in-law. A citizen who came out to get them after the coyote dumped them."

Eleanda raised a hand, laughed. "OK. OK. You did just what I would have done. I kept doing it until one day I got shot at. After that I'd call a backup even if it was an old lady in a wheelchair carrying a baby."

"All right then," Bernie said. "Sorry I sounded so grouchy. You think Mr. Henry will get on me about this?"

"You betcha. But if this is the first time he got on you about something it'll just be about a five-minute lecture. Little bit of finger shaking, and a couple of 'Goddammits,' and a 'Don't let it happen again.' Will this be the first time on the carpet?"

"Well," Bernie said. "I guess so. But he called me in about getting onto the Tuttle Ranch. I didn't know we had that special deal with them."

Eleanda's eyebrows rose. "I didn't either. What deal?"

"Mr. Henry said they do our work for us on the ranch. You know, tipping us off if illegals show up. Sort of unofficially holding them until we come to the gate and take custody. And in return we don't go in their hunting preserve, or get nosey if they have their rich Mexican business friends in there on hunting trips."

Eleanda had taken orange juice out of the refrigerator and was pouring herself a glass.

"Nobody told me about that," she said. "But maybe because it's sort of, shall we say, semi-illegal. Or an exception not provided for by the statutes." She laughed. "One of those arrangements that takes days of writing reports if the wrong people hear about it."

"Eleanda," Bernie said, "why would Mr. Henry want to take a picture of me?"

Eleanda looked surprised. "I can't imagine. When did that happen?"

"I took some photos out at the Tuttle place. Oryx, and the Mexican truck I followed in there, things like that. And Mr. Henry told me to turn them over to him. And then he said he had to have a photo of me. And he took one."

Eleanda shook her head. "Maybe because he likes your looks. You're a good-looking woman. But, really, I don't know. Didn't he say."

"Just that he needed it."

Eleanda was studying Bernie over her glass of orange juice. "You're worried about this?"

Bernie debated what to tell Eleanda, noticed the woman's concern, decided to tell her everything.

"This man who was picking up the illegals. Delos Vasquez. The dispatcher said someone of that name might have worked for the dopers at Agua Prieta. He said he recognized me. That they had a picture of me at Agua Prieta."

"Who had it?"

"He said people in the drug trade. Said he'd driven for them a while and then quit because he was afraid of them."

Eleanda was thinking, frowning. She nodded. "He was trying to make a hit on you, Bernie. You're a good-looking woman. Most likely, he just made it up. Or it could have been a picture of someone else."

"He said he thought he recognized me right away, and then he knew it was me because of that little silver pin of mine. Big Thunder. I had it on my shirt collar. And I was wearing it when Henry took the picture."

"On your uniform shirt?"

Bernie nodded.

"I'll bet he didn't like that."

"Henry told me it was against the rules to wear jewelry on duty."

"But you had it on yesterday."

"It's for good luck," Bernie said.

Eleanda finished the orange juice. Looked pensive. "Why would they hand your photo around among the coyotes at Agua Prieta. Did this Vasquez explain that?"

Bernie looked embarrassed. "He said they were supposed to be on the lookout for me. Be afraid of me."

Eleanda considered this, abruptly reached a decision.

"Have you talked to Sergeant Chee about this? If you haven't you should."

"Why?"

"Because he's a cop with a lot better connection than us. See if he can find out what's going on."

Bernie didn't respond to that.

"Have you told Henry about it?"

Bernie shook her head.

"I wouldn't. He's the one who took the picture, and I sometimes think . . . Well, I'm not sure about him. Call your sergeant. See what he thinks."

"He'll think I'm silly."

"He won't," Eleanda said. "And if you don't call him, I will."

Bernie stared at her, bit her lip.

"Honey, time to get smart. That man hurt your feelings. But he really likes you."

"Oh, yeah," Bernie said. "He also likes stray cats, and retarded kids, and . . ."

"OK, then. I'll call him."

Bernie grimaced. "OK then. But if you think it's something dangerous we should know more about, call Joe Leaphorn. He's retired, but he knows everybody. He'd do what he could."

And so, Bernie gave Leaphorn's number to Mrs. Garza.

17

Leaphorn was out in his driveway searching his car for a notebook he had left somewhere.

"Joe!" Louisa Bourbonette shouted. "Telephone."

"Can you take a number. Tell 'em I'll call 'em. I want to find these notes."

"It's long distance. A woman named Garza. From Rodeo, wherever that is."

Leaphorn hustled up the walk, said thanks, took the phone, said, "This is Joe Leaphorn."

"I'm Eleanda Garza. A Customs patrol officer with the Border Patrol. And I'm Bernadette Manuelito's housemate. I think you're a friend of hers."

"I am," Leaphorn said. "Is she all right?"

"Fine. Just homesick and lonesome. But she

had some information she wanted me to pass along to you."

Mrs. Garza thereupon started at the beginning. Bernie taking the pictures at the Tuttle Ranch of the exotic animals and the work project. Ed Henry, her supervisor, telling her she had violated an arrangement Customs had with the ranch, described the arrangement, described Henry photographing Bernie, told of Bernie arresting the four illegals and their driver and how the driver had recognized Bernie—telling her that drug operators in Agua Prieta had copies of the photo Henry had taken, and they had the idea that Bernie was some sort of special agent for the Drug Enforcement Agency.

Halfway through this account Leaphorn sat himself on the car's fender, but he didn't interrupt.

"Any questions?" Mrs. Garza asked.

"Not until you're finished," he said.

"I am."

"OK. How do you know Mr. Henry took the photograph?"

Garza explained.

"And these illegals, were they in the drug traffic?"

"The driver told Bernie he had been, in a

minor way. Some driving for them but he'd been afraid, and quit."

"How about the other four?"

She described them with names, and their reasons for immigrating after failing to find work at the old smelter.

"That smelter. At San Pedro de los Corralitos, I think you said. You know anything about that?"

"Not much. I think it was running all through World War II when the price was so high and then on into the 1960s until the price went down. And the old man, Mr. Gomez, said there were rumors it was reopening and hiring people. I had heard those rumors, too. My aunt wrote me about them way last year. She said everybody thought there would be jobs again, but nothing was happening."

"You have family down there?"

Mrs. Garza laughed. "I have family all over Sonora. Garzas, and Tapias, and Montoyas. I was a Tapia, and my great-uncle Jorge Tapia, he ran one of the furnaces there at San Pedro de los Corralitos for Anaconda when they had the smelter. But then they sold it to Phelps Dodge and he got laid off. But that was when I was a little girl. Now my aunt said another company had bought it, and everybody thought the mine there would open again and the smelter would be hiring. But no." Mrs. Garza paused, inhaled, sighed.

"That didn't happen?"

"She said a crew came in to dig up part of that old gas line and fixed it up. One of my nephews did some of the dirt moving. But they brought in their own pipeline people to do the technical work. And the jobs just lasted a few weeks."

"All they were doing was fixing a pipeline?"

"He said they replaced some of the broken windows in a storage building. Cleaned up stuff. Things like that."

"What can you tell me about the pipeline?"

"All I know about that is it must be the one that brought in the gas for the fires in the smelter. To melt down the ore. Or whatever they do. My aunt said people were happy about that. What would they need gas for if they weren't going to get the smelter going again?" She sighed once more.

"One final question. Do you know I'm retired. Not with the police anymore? Why are you telling me this?"

"How do I answer that?" Garza said. "I guess I just tell you the truth. I told Bernie she should call her Sergeant Chee, her former boss, and see if he could figure out what it was all about. But she wouldn't call him. Said you knew everybody in law enforcement out here. You'd be better, and you'd be willing to help."

"I will help if I can," Leaphorn said.

"I also think Bernie would be happy if you passed all that information along to her sergeant."

"I'll do that," Leaphorn said.

"Oh," Garza said. "But don't tell him I said Bernie said you'd be better."

"I won't," Leaphorn said.

And that was pretty much the end of the conversation. Leaphorn slid off the fender and rubbed his ear.

Louisa reached for the phone.

"Thanks," Leaphorn said, but he kept the telephone.

"You said you'd help if you could. How?"

"I don't know," Leaphorn said.

"And what do you mean, just saying 'Thanks'? What was that all about? Is Bernie all right? From the way you were looking, it sounded pretty serious."

"I don't know," Leaphorn said. "Maybe it is." And he told Louisa why he thought so.

"I think you should do something about this," Louisa said. "If you can think of what in the world you can do. At least tell Jim Chee about it."

"Leaphorn was punching keys on the cell phone. "I'm doing that now," he said. But he stopped dialing.

"Louisa, you're good at finding the stuff I'm always misplacing. Now I've got to find what I've done with some old maps. U.S. Geological Survey, or Bureau of Indian Affairs, or maybe Bureau of Land Management, or Department of Energy. I remember having at least two that showed major pipeline routes and one of them even included lines where the government had granted easements for pipeline rights."

"I think you keep the old, old maps you no longer look at but are too stubborn to throw away in that big cardboard box on the shelf in the garage," Louisa said. "And since you're already all dusty from hunting whatever you lost in the car I'll let you climb up and get it down yourself."

18

Winsor's trip to solve the Mexican end of his problem took many preparations. He called his man at the bank and sent Budge down with a check and a note, thereby withdrawing a bundle of Mexican currency to have with him in case it was needed on the border or in Sonora. He made a call to his congressman's office to get the doer of helpful deeds there to ease the way with Customs officials and set things up for Budge to get international flight permissions cleared for his Dessault Falcon 10 to enter and leave Mexico. With competent assistants on call, political clout, and deep pockets, he had no problems getting such jobs rapidly accomplished. First stop would be El Paso, where he'd told his Mexican lawyer to meet him. His next stop would depend on what he learned in that conversation.

Meanwhile, he would spend the flight time improving his understanding of Budge. The competence with which Budge had dealt with Chrissy hadn't surprised him. But the coolness of the man and his utter confidence in himself had suggested to Winsor that there was a depth to Budge he hadn't expected. Before long he expected Chrissy's many girlfriends and her family would be wondering what happened, why no one was answering her telephone, why his own secretary didn't know why she wasn't showing up for work, why her professors out at the university law school knew nothing at all. Pretty soon her family would report her missing, he'd be getting questions. The police would be making inquiries.

Chrissy's family were Italian immigrants operating a string of restaurants. They had political connections in their state. They weren't the sort he wanted to socialize with in Washington or New York, but they were useful with one senator and three of their state's congressmen. That meant almost certainly the Washington police would be on the hunt, probably the FBI as well.

He had worried about that. Braced himself for unpleasantness. But Budge had worked it out so that the story left behind would be too simple to interest either the press or the police. She had called for the limo, told Budge she had to go to the airport, he had taken her there, left her off at her airline's terminal as she requested, and come home. And thus Chrissy, and the threat she represented, had vanished without a trace. Budge had left absolutely nothing for police or press to find. A real cool professional at work.

Winsor found himself thinking of this immigrant Latino as a man of his own class, just as he thought of the top people with whom he dined, and partied, and competed with in the economic and political world. That sort of thinking surprised him. He never felt that way about his employees. On one level, he felt good about this. On another, it made him uneasy. It undercut his trust. He no longer felt totally safe in presuming, as he had been doing, that Budge was simply a highly competent lackey, happy to be serving in a job that paid him well. Now Budge seemed more than that. Perhaps he wasn't—as Haret had always seemed to be—one of those little suckerfish that connects itself to sharks.

Maybe Budge had his own predatory talents. Worse, maybe Budge had his own personal agenda.

At the airport he found Budge waiting in the lounge for private aircraft crews. He was reading a magazine, looking comfortable.

"We'll probably have to spend a night or two out where we won't find hotel accommodations," Winsor said. "Are you prepared for that?"

"Always am," Budge said. "Bed roll in the storage space and some U.S. Army canned rations. How about you? Will I be sharing my food?"

"I'll make other arrangements," Winsor said. "I'll be meeting some associates."

Budge considered that, nodded.

"I'll sit up front with you," he told Budge as they boarded the jet. "I want to talk to you."

"Why?" Budge asked.

"Just curious," Winsor said. "I'm paying your salary. I'm putting some confidence in you. So I need to know more about you."

"You know the rule," Budge said. "Passengers will please refrain from talking to the driver."

"I make the rules," Winsor said.

Budge studied him, expressionless. He nodded. "When we get to altitude and we get into the flight pattern, then we will talk," he said. "Until then, I'll be talking only to the tower. You can listen."

Judging from what Winsor was seeing of the landscape, they were over West Virginia before Budge turned toward him: "All right. Now what do you want to know."

"We could start with your biography," Winsor said. "All I know about you is what the congressman told me. You flew for the government in that messy rebellion in Guatemala. You got in some sort of trouble. You had connections in the CIA down there and they got you to Washington. That about right?"

Budge considered, said: "That's about it."

"I'm not even sure I know your real name. 'Robert Budge' doesn't sound like you. That doesn't seem to fit what you look like."

Budge thought about this. "That does sound a little pale for me, I guess. How about Sylvanius Roberto C. de Baca. That sound right?"

"'Sylvanius'? That sounds Greek. But that 'C. de Baca' sounds Spanish."

"It is Spanish," Budge said. "Or technically

Basque, I guess. It's my father's name. He was one of those freedom fighters who gave Franco and his fascists troubles."

"What's the 'C'? Maybe Carlos?"

"'C' is short for 'Cabeza.' Cabeza de Baca."

"I had a high school course in Spanish. Doesn't **cabeza** mean 'head'? Is that 'Head of Baca'?" Winsor snorted. "And 'Baca.' What's that? Come on, Budge, get with it. I don't have time to play games with you."

"When you studied Spanish, they didn't get into history much, I guess. Anyway, back in the fifteenth century, when the Castilians were fighting that long civil war to drive the Moors out of Spain, the king gave my family that name. A grandfather of mine, six centuries removed, led a scouting party to find a way the Spanish army"—Budge paused, looked at Winsor—"you familiar with Spanish geography, lay of the land?"

Winsor felt himself flushing. He wasn't accustomed to this.

"I've never had a reason to be," he said.

"I'll make it simple then. He found a way for the army of the king to get a column of cavalry across a river where they could outflank the Moors. That won the war for our side.

According to the legend, my ancestor marked the ford with the skull of a cow stuck up on the end of a pole. After the Moors surrendered, the king had a ceremonial banquet in the palace and made this very distant granddad of mine Duke of Cabeza de Baca."

Winsor laughed. "Maybe they ate the beef from the historic baca's cabeza."

Budge cut off what he was about to say to that, paused, adjusted something on the instrument panel.

"That was fourteen hundred and thirteen. Long, long ago," he said, and laughed. "About when the early Winsors would have still been gathering roots and berries, eating with their fingers and killing each other with clubs."

Winsor took a deep breath, held it, and stared out the windshield. "Interesting," he said after a long silence. "About all I know about the Spanish culture is from Cervante's novels, and the plays the Spanish dramatists were writing about that time and the stuff we got in the world lit classes at Harvard. Now, tell me what brought the Cabeza de Baca family to the Americas."

"Spirit of adventure. Lust for gold. Hard times in Europe. The same old story. I think my ancestors had a habit of being on the wrong side of too many political battles."

"What did you do for the CIA?" Winsor's question produced a long silence.

"One thing I would have been required to do, if I ever did work for the Central Intelligence Agency, was put my hand on a Bible and take an oath of secrecy. So if I did that, I can't talk about it. And if I didn't do that, then there'd be nothing to tell you. Right?"

A long silence ensued.

"When we get about an hour from El Paso, I'm making some calls," Winsor said. "You take care of dealing with getting my plane parked. I'll meet a man I need to talk to at the administration building. You brought your cell phone?"

"Always. And the pager."

"Stay close to the plane. I'll call you when I need you."

"Sure," Budge said.

They crossed the American midlands in silence. Over the flatness of West Texas Winsor extracted his cell phone and dialed. He waited, looking impatient.

"Ruben? . . . Yes, yes. Did our lawyer show up? . . . Yes, at the airport. You talk to the people at Rancho Corralitos? . . . Yes . . . yes, but that

means the stuff hasn't actually arrived there yet.
. . . True? But when? . . . That sounds all right.
But you make damn sure nothing holds it up.
Tell me how you're checking on it."

The answer to that took time. Winsor
glanced at Budge, who seemed to be absorbed
with reading his instrument panel.

"All right then. But call me as soon as it's
there. And I'm thinking now that we'll be coming right on in from El Paso this afternoon.
Make damn sure that landing strip is cleaned off
better than it was the last time. And I'll probably have to spend the night. Where we're going
next we can't land in the dark. And did those
Corralitos people have anything new to say
about that woman?"

A brief pause. "What woman? The snoopy
Navajo gal that was nosing around at the Pig
Trap site, taking pictures. We had her picture
spread around."

Winsor listened. Said: "Son of a bitch! Did
you ask Ed Henry about that?" Listened again.
Shook his head, said: "How did Henry know the
man was a Navajo." Said: "I mean, how did he
know he was a Navajo Tribal Police cop. They
don't have any jurisdiction down there. None at
all." He listened again, said: "All right," and

clicked off without saying good-bye. He put the phone back in his jacket pocket and glanced at Budge.

"You need to be ready to fly on to the smelter. Take care of refueling if you need to, as soon as we get landed."

Budge nodded.

"We need to get there before dark," Budge said. "I'm not going to fly in on that strip by starlight."

While he was saying that, Winsor was staring at him, expression thoughtful.

"Budge," he said. "You sort of enjoyed that assignment I gave you with Chrissy, didn't you? I mean, manhandling that pretty little girl like that."

Budge kept his eyes on the instrument panel, shrugged.

"I think I'm going to have another one of those for you," Winsor said.

Budge considered that a moment. "Who?"

Winsor chuckled. "It may not be so easy this time. She's some sort of cop."

19

The young woman who answered Leaphorn's call to Jim Chee's Shiprock office recognized neither his voice nor his name, making him aware of the passage of time, how old he was getting, how long he had been retired, how quickly one is forgotten, and other sad truths. But when he identified himself more clearly and told her the call was important, she said that while Sergeant Chee had indeed left for the day and wasn't in his office, he still might be out in the parking lot. She went out to see.

A minute later, Chee was on the phone and asking what was up.

"Get comfortable, Jim," Leaphorn said. "This takes a while to tell."

Being Leaphorn, he had his thoughts about as well organized as this peculiar and disconnected affair allowed. He started with Mrs. Garza's call.

"I think we know from the photo Henry took of Bernie Manuelito that all is not totally well with Customs operations down there," Leaphorn said. "How else would the photograph get into the hands of the drug people down in Sonora? But why would they consider Miss Manuelito dangerous? It seems obvious, at least to me, that it had to do with her photographing whatever they're building on the Tuttle Ranch. What do you think about it?"

"I don't have any ideas," Chee said. "I'm going down there and get her out of it."

Leaphorn laughed. "Better take along a court order and your handcuffs. It always seemed to me that Bernie Manuelito pretty much made her own decisions."

"Well, yes," Chee said. "She does. But if I tell her—"

"There's more I want to explain," Leaphorn said. "I want you to take a look at an old map I dug up."

Now Chee snorted. "A map! Have I ever discussed anything with you when you didn't pull a map on me?"

"It's a different one this time," Leaphorn

said. "I think the U.S. Geological Survey did it back in 1950 on the national energy distribution system. Pipelines and electrical transmission grids, all that."

"Pipelines," Chee said. "Ah. Are we getting into what happened to the Indian Trust Fund oil and gas royalty money?"

"Possibly," Leaphorn said. "Could we get together? And where would be a good place for you?"

"I need to go to Window Rock, anyway," Chee said. "How about this evening?"

When Professor Louisa Bourbonette answered the doorbell and ushered him into the kitchen, Leaphorn was sitting at the table. Two maps spread across it and more were stacked on a chair.

Leaphorn waved Chee to sit.

"Need I ask if you'd like coffee," said Louisa. The pot was already steaming, and she took three mugs from the cabinet.

"Part of this I haven't been able to work out yet," Leaphorn said, pointing to the larger of the maps. "But the southern end works out beautifully."

"Meaning what?" Chee said, pulling his chair closer and leaning in for a look.

"Here we have the location of that abandoned Mexican copper smelter," Leaphorn said,
tapping the map with his pencil. "San Pedro de
los Corralles on this old map, and this symbol
is—I should say was—the Anaconda Copper
Corporation's San Pedro smelter when this map
was drawn. The newer maps"—he indicated the
maps on the chair beside him—"they don't
show either the village or the smelter. Nor the
pipe that brought the smelter its fuel from the
San Juan Basin fields. However, look at the old
map. And remember, abandoned pipelines are
normally just left where they were buried.
Digging them up costs more than they're
worth."

Leaphorn glanced up at Chee as he said this,
and put the pencil tip on a line of dashes that
ran northward from the smokestack symbol of
the smelter. The line was labeled "EPNG," the
acronym for El Paso Natural Gas Company. It
followed a narrow valley east of the Guadalupe
Mountain range in Mexico's state of Sonora and
crossed the U.S. border into the Playas Valley of
New Mexico. Leaphorn ran the pencil tip along
the route, following it through the Hatchet Gap,
which separated the Big Hatchet Mountains
from the Little Hatchets. In the Hatchita Valley

east of the gap he marked a tiny "X" and looked up at Chee.

"Does that just about mark the place on the Tuttle Ranch where Bernie took those pictures?"

Chee nodded. "I'd think that would be awfully close to where Bernie saw them working."

"Anyway," Leaphorn said, "if this old map is accurate and if the folks in the county courthouses in Luna and Hidalgo Counties gave me the correct legal description of the Tuttle Ranch property, then the old pipeline runs right through that ranch."

"This is getting very interesting," Chee said. "Do you know anything about the Tuttle family background?"

"The county clerk at Deming said the ownership changed three years ago. Now the owner of record is a Delaware Corporation. Some sort of holding company, I guess. A.G.H. Industries. Ever hear of it?"

"Never," Chee said. "So you're thinking the folks Bernie saw working there were digging down to the old pipeline. Making some sort of connection. It would be empty, now, wouldn't it? What would be the purpose?"

"Before I give you my guess at that let's shift

over to my new and updated copy of that Triple A Indian Country map." Leaphorn pulled it over on top of the USGS map. Chee noticed he'd already marked an "X" on the Tuttle Ranch and another "X" up at the edge of the Jicarilla Reservation about where the body of the so-called Carl Mankin had been found.

"I see you've made the connection," Chee said. "From a junked copper smelter down in Sonora all the way up to our Four Corners homicide. Aren't we stretching that old pipeline too far?"

"I don't know," Leaphorn said. "Maybe we are. Anyway, it probably stretched that far once. Anaconda was using San Juan Basin gas to fire that smelter."

"I'm guessing you've already done some checking on that historic end of it."

"Some," Leaphorn said. "I called an old Anaconda man down in Silver City. He said that before he retired they were getting their gas from EPNG out of the San Juan field. And now I'm told some construction is going on there, but not involving smelting copper."

"So you've used the old pipeline to get the Mankin killing connected to whatever goes on at Tuttle Ranch and whatever's happening down in

Sonora." Chee shook his head. "I'm way behind you on that connection."

Louisa had poured their coffee, a mug for herself, joined them at the table, but had politely refrained from getting into this discussion. Now she cleared her throat.

"Of course he's behind, Joe. Who wouldn't be? Tell him about your pig theory." She smiled at Chee. "As Joe sees this situation these are very sinister pigs."

Leaphorn looked slightly embarrassed.

"Pig is the name pipeline maintenance people use for a device they push through the pipes to clean them out. First they were simply a cylinder that fit the dimensions of the pipeline and was short enough, or flexible enough, to make it around corners and ups and downs in the line. They were covered with pig bristle to brush away rust and deposits. These days they've gotten much more high-tech. Computer chips in them, sensing devices and transmitters so they can measure wear, find cracks, let management know where repairs need be made, so forth."

Chee was considering this, surveying what he knew about pipelines, which was virtually nothing. He'd heard that the major lines sometimes were moving several products at the same time, like miles of crude oil, followed by refined gasoline, followed by methane gas, or something else. He presumed some sort of barrier was used to separate the products. But how? And how were these products moved along, and taken out? If it wasn't gravity-driven, it must require some sort of pumping. Putting pressure in the line to push whatever was in it along. But he'd never really given it any thought.

"So," he said, "are you thinking they're using the old pipeline to smuggle something in. Like dope, perhaps. Or nuclear devices for Al Qaeda's terrorism campaign, to slip radioactive stuff past radiation detectors. Or maybe to smuggle something out of the country."

"Take your pick," Leaphorn said. "Whichever it is, I think something illegal must be involved. And it's pretty clear some very big money is operating here. Buying the ranch, paying for that construction, making some investments here and there to make sure the Mexican police aren't interfering."

"And big money makes it dangerous," Chee said. "I mean for anyone who interferes. Like Bernie. You remember how she tended to get involved in things without being told to."

Leaphorn nodded. "And apparently some-one believes our Miss Manuelito may be doing that now."

Louisa exhaled abruptly, producing a sound that signaled frustrated impatience.

"I can't believe this," she said. "You two sitting here, perfectly calm, discussing the mechanics of pipelines, and convincing yourselves that Bernadette Manuelito is in danger of being killed."

Leaphorn stared at her. So did Chee.

"Instead of doing what?" Leaphorn asked. "You want us to kidnap her and bring her home?"

Louisa's expression was disapproving. "Well, you should do something. If you have it figured correctly, you think they—whoever they are—have already killed that man . . . that homicide up by the Jicarilla Reservation."

"Yes," Chee said.

"Let's see what we have," Leaphorn said. "No evidence a crime is being committed. We have no jurisdiction if there is a crime. We have no—"

"No common sense either," she said. "Sergeant Chee knows very well that if he went down there he could get Bernie out of that mess. Bring her home."

Chee put down his coffee cup, leaned forward.

"Jurisdiction," he said. "Isn't most of that land down in the New Mexico boot heel public domain land? Government owned and just leased out to the ranchers?"

"Ah," Leaphorn said. "I see what you're thinking. I'll call the county clerk at Deming. She'll know how much of that ranch is under lease."

"I don't see what Jim's thinking," said Louisa. "Let me in on this."

"He's thinking that if that construction site Bernie photographed on the Tuttle Ranch is on public domain land, even a Bureau of Land Management enforcement officer would have a perfectly valid legal right to go in there and make an inspection. Right?"

"Right," Chee said. "At least I think so."

"If you can find one to do it for you," Leaphorn said.

"You remember Cowboy Dashee, don't you, Lieutenant. That Hopi friend of mine who was an Apache County deputy. Well, he's now an officer with the BLM enforcement division."

Leaphorn got out of his chair.

"I'll call Deming," he said. "You see if you

can find Officer Dashee. And we'll want to get Officer Bernadette Manuelito in on this, too."

"If she's already in on it, I want to get her out of it," Chee said. "I'm going to find Cowboy. Get him involved in this business."

20

Bureau of Land Management Enforcement Officer Cowboy Dashee's schedule of duties for the next few days included investigating a controversy about overgrazing on the fringe of the Carson National Forest, reports of an unauthorized fence on another grazing lease, and illegal diversion of snowmelt runoff from a stream into a stock pond. All of these involved leased federal land along the New Mexico–Colorado border. As Cowboy was telling Jim Chee, that's a hell of a long way from the Tuttle Ranch.

"I know," Chee said. "But think of the glory you get if you break up some sort of smuggling scheme. Like diversion of our crude oil—or maybe natural gas—out of the country without taxes or royalties paid. Or smuggling in nuclear devices where radiation detectors can't sense them. Or heroin. Or cocaine. Any of that stuff."

"You think about that. I'll think about the trouble I'll have lying out of it if this just turns out to be a Navajo pipe dream. And here I am, marginal jurisdiction at best, no evidence, no clues, just this funny story about piping dope into the country through an abandoned gas line."

"Tell 'em we had a tip that the Islamic terrorists were going to start sending nuclear bombs through the pipe to blow up the J. Edgar Hoover building in Washington," Chee said. "They'd like that."

"In a rusty old pipeline?" Dashee said. "I don't think those bombs would go off. And if they're sending pot through, I don't think I'd want to smoke it." He laughed. "They couldn't call the coke they shipped that way nose candy."

"Those pipes don't rust much," Chee said. "Not in dry country they don't. Built to last forever."

Dashee considered this. They were standing beside his official federal vehicle—a Dodge Ram pickup wearing the BLM insignia—at his little stone house at the outskirts of Walpi on the

Hopi Second Mesa. He was staring south as if, Chee thought, Cowboy could see two hundred or so miles south and east into New Mexico's boot heel desert country to where he hoped Dashee would soon be taking them. Chee gave him some time to think, uneasy, but enjoying the view.

Walpi was on the high edge of the mesa, maybe seven thousand feet above sea level and a couple of thousand feet above the immensity of empty country below them. A truck was rolling down U.S. 264 far below their feet, ant-sized, and the thunderheads of the late-summer monsoon season were beginning to build over Tovar Mesa, and the Hopi Buttes, and the ragged spire of Montezuma's Chair miles to the south. No lightning yet, and only one of the clouds was dragging a mist of vigara below it. As the cloud towers rose higher later in the morning some of them would make rain. Now they only produced a pattern of cloud shadows dappling the landscape dark blue as they drifted eastward.

Dashee sighed. "You're sure about this photo of Bernie?" he asked. "It was taken by her boss, and it was handed around to some druggies in Sonora. I mean, right away after it was taken? And the word from there was that they think Bernie is dangerous?" He stared at Chee. "Is that true? Not just speculation?"

Chee nodded.

"You're a hell of a lot of trouble. My folks always warned me about associating with you Head Breakers."

"No more head breaking," Chee said. "Now we Navajos kill folks with our kindness."

"Head Breakers" was a pejorative Hopi term for Navajos, the traditional enemies of the Hopi since about the sixteenth century. It suggested Dashee's tribe considered them too unsophisticated to invent bows and arrows.

"You're telling me Lieutenant Leaphorn believes all this nonsense too," Dashee said. "The Legendary Lieutenant is endorsing this."

"He's the one who figured it out. Found the pipeline on one of his maps."

"Oh, well," Dashee said. "We better take my truck then. If we're going to be busting in on these people, we want to make it look official."

"I'd say head east over to Gallup, then south through the Zuñi Reservation to Fence Lake, then State Road 36 through Quemado, and then down to Lordsburg. Get a motel there, be up early and . . ."

Dashee was glowering at him.

"I see you already have my route all planned. You took ole Cowboy for granted again." Dashee shifted into his copy of Chee's voice: "'Just go on over to Second Mesa and get Cowboy. He's easy. He'll believe whatever you tell him.'"

"Ah, come on Cowboy. You know—"

"Just kidding," Cowboy said. "Let's go."

"I owe you one," Chee said.

"One?" Cowboy said. "You already owe me about six."

21

Budge got Winsor's Falcon 10 jet ready to fly and reassured himself that arrangements had been properly made to clear this journey into Mexico. Then he found a comfortable chair in the transient flights waiting room and sat trying to decide what to do. Progress on that was slow. Memories of Chrissy kept intruding.

The first time he'd met her, almost the first moment in fact, she had made him aware that she was not the usual type of young woman Winsor sent him to collect. He'd been following his standard limo driver pattern, arriving about fifteen minutes early, waiting about ten minutes, and then ringing the bell and announcing that he was early but available at her convenience. But this time Chrissy had spoken first.

"Oh, my," she had said. "I'm sorry. I'm sorry I'm late. I'll hurry. I'll be right down."

The young women Winsor had previously collected had without any exceptions actually been late, had never apologized, had never hurried, and had never shown any interest in whether he minded waiting out in the frosty darkness. They were so far away on the upper side of the class barrier that limo drivers were invisible to them. They showed no more interest in who was driving the car than they would for the spare tire in the trunk. The first few times he'd done this chore, he had ventured a friendly welcome, or one of those "nice evening" remarks. The responses, if any, had been cool and terse, letting him know that it was pushy and intrusive of him to dare to speak to a debutante from whichever expensive and exclusive finishing school had finished them.

Chrissy had been different. She had hurried out of the apartment house entry and reached the car in such a rush that she'd had her hand on the door handle before he could get there to open it for her.

"Golly," she said. "I'm sorry I've kept you waiting. My dad taught us that being late is really rude. It tells the other person you think you're more important than they are."

"Actually, I was a little early," Budge had said. And when they were en route he ventured a "nice evening" remark. This time it had touched off a conversation. Chrissy actually introduced herself to him. And so it had gone. During the dozens of times he'd been her driver since that day, they'd become friends in a strange sort of way, answering one another's biographical questions, exchanging opinions of current Washingtonian uproars and controversies, agreeing that this city was interesting but had more than its share of people way, way too driven by greed and ambition. And gradually it became more and more personal.

"I guess I'm one of those greedy ones, too," Chrissy had said one day. "I came here to try to get into law school at George Washington University, and I did, so now I'm in it, and making good grades, and I'm surrounded by lawyers. And by law students. And all they seem to think about is either getting money or getting power. And I'm not sure anymore I want to be one."

"Yeah," Budge had said. "I used to be a political activist. 'Power to the People,' you know. Or, as we used to shout over in Catalonia when I was a kid, **'A la pared por los ricos'**—'Firing squad for the rich folks.' Dreamed of being the czar of the universe. I was going to reform everything, start with the soccer rules, work up to the United Nations, and then see what I could do with human nature."

"But no more?" she asked. "Did you give up on all that?" Her voice sounded sad, but maybe that was just to play along with his joke.

"It was just a dream," he said. "My family was always on the wrong side, from the fight against Franco and the fascists to running to South America and getting with the losing side down there."

"Well, now you're a success. You're making a lot of money," she said. "I know you're not just getting paid to drive the limo. You're sort of an aide to Mr. Winsor. I've heard him talking about you."

"And what did he say?"

"Well, once I heard him tell Mr. Haret, the man who works with Congress for him, he told him that you were the only one he had he could absolutely count on. And on the telephone once, he was telling someone that when things get out of control he turns it over to Budge, and he knows Budge will fix it."

"Did he mention why he can depend on me?"

"No," she said, then hesitated. "Unless he said you owed him a great big favor. Maybe that was it."

"It was."

"So what was the favor?"

"Let's see," Budge said. "How can I explain it. It gets very complicated. But I guess the bottom line is he keeps me from being deported, and that keeps me out of jail."

"I don't understand," she said. "How does he do that?"

He sighed. "Here's where the complexity comes in. In Guatemala, and other places like that, the Central Intelligence Agency uses people like me, sort of off the record, and when things go wrong they get some of them out, somewhere safe, or maybe even into the United States. Arrange papers for them so they can get lost in the crowd. All quietly, no papers signed, nobody admitting anything. So if I started telling my story—not that it's very interesting— to the newspapers, or if someone else did and some committee called me to testify about what

happened down there, the CIA would swear
they never heard of me, and nobody could prove
otherwise."

"Oh," Chrissy said, sounding thoughtful.
"But how does Mr. Winsor keep you from being
deported?"

"By keeping his mouth shut," Budge said.

Chrissy produced one of those "what do you
mean by that" looks.

Budge considered how to explain. "Let's say
I was no longer a true and faithful servant and
became more trouble than I was worth. Mr.
Winsor is now keeping me from being deported
very simply. Just not tipping off the Immigration
folks, or by refraining from telling one of his
lawyer friends in the State Department that the
people now running my former country have a
warrant out for me under my former name. If he
wanted me deported, he'd simply make a telephone call to the right person."

Silence. Then she said: "Oh, I'm sorry. I
shouldn't be so nosey."

"No offense taken," Budge said.

"I can't believe you did anything very
wrong."

"Well, I guess you could say I haven't been a

great benefactor for society," Budge said, and laughed.

"Don't laugh at yourself. Anyway, you're fine now. Good job, good prospects. I get the impression that Mr. Winsor will be putting you in charge of things. There'd be a lot more money with that."

"The Beatles taught us about money. Remember? It won't buy you love."

"Her response to that sounded slightly angry.

"You like to make fun of money," she said. "I have to tell you I don't. I bet you've never been poor or you wouldn't talk like that. I bet you've never had to watch your mother trying to borrow money, or been embarrassed in school because of the way you dressed. Or your shoes. Or hearing the other girls telling about what they did during the summer, and all you could do was listen. Things like that."

"No," Budge said. "Never anything like that."

"Well, I have," she said. "You dream of having money. Like dreaming of paradise. Having money like those people I see when I'm with Rawley."

All the anger was out of her voice now. It sounded dreamy.

"Listening to them talking about the party in Tokyo. Or being on somebody's yacht going up the Thames. Being introduced to the Queen. The view from somebody's villa on the cliff in Sicily. The candlesticks. The silver." She stopped, sighed. "Oh, well. Maybe someday."

Winsor's other young women had never talked like that. One sunny Saturday afternoon when he picked up Chrissy he'd been tempted to tell her about the very blond, very chic, very shapely girl he had delivered to the Winsor address two days earlier. Just make a casual remark about it. See how Chrissy would respond. To learn if she understood how she fit into Winsor's scheme of things and knew what was happening to her. But he didn't tell her. He told himself he didn't tell her because it would have been cruel to tip her off if she didn't know and insulting if she did. But the real reason he was silent was that he was afraid it would destroy this friendship. And he had come to treasure that.

Then the day came, about a month ago, just as he started the limo engine and was pulling away from the curb, when Chrissy clicked on the intercom and said:

"Budge. I think I'm pregnant."

That surprised him. It shouldn't have, perhaps. But it did. And he said nothing at all for a bit, and then he said, "Oh?"

"We're going to get married. Rawley's given me an engagement ring. It's spectacular. I'd show it to you, but I can't wear it yet. This is going to be secret until he can get his divorce finalized and the wedding arrangements made."

And he'd said: "Well, Chrissy, I wish you a lot of happiness." And he'd wondered why he hadn't heard about this impending divorce. From what he'd been hearing, Winsor was still solidly married to a very socially prominent woman named Margo Lodge Winsor. He'd driven her out to Reagan Airport about two months ago on a flight to their vacation home in the Antilles. He'd never been sent out to pick her up, and Winsor had talked a time or two about his plans for joining her there.

He had no idea what, if anything, to say to Chrissy about that, and a damper fell on their friendly chats for a couple of their trips. But then came that terrible day that forced him to make some decisions.

Budge was remembering that day now, just as Winsor arrived and stood looking down at him.

"Up and at 'em," Winsor said. "Get moving. You've got the plane ready, I trust. Everything all set?"

"For where?" he said, not moving.

"For the old smelter in Sonora," Winsor said. "Come on. You're wasting my time."

Budge looked at his boot tips, then up at Winsor. "OK," he said. "Away we go."

The flight from El Paso's Biggs Field to the old smelter is a mere hundred and fifty or so air miles over a stretch of the emptiest segment of Chihuahua to the emptiest part of Sonora. Dry country, relatively flat, and the pilot's role complicated only by the chance of encountering the helicopters and radio-controlled drone surveillance aircraft the Border Patrol uses to watch the bottom edge of New Mexico and Arizona.

Winsor sat behind him now, silent, reading papers in a folder. Budge identified the bumpy shape of Sierra Alto Azul Mountain, his navigating mark for the smelter, adjusted his controls, and looked at the desert below him. Grim, dry, hungry, unhappy country, not intended for any life beyond javlina, cactus wrens, and reptiles. Too harsh and cruel for humans, and that returned his thoughts to the last time he'd seen Chrissy, the afternoon Winsor had summoned him into that luxurious office, asked him to sit down—a first for that—and offered him a cigar, which was another first.

"Budge," he'd said, "I've been thinking of the things you've managed for me. Four years now, isn't it, and you've never let me down."

"Four years," Budge said. "I guess that's about right."

"I'm going to give you a bonus," Winsor said. He was smiling.

"A pay raise?"

"No. Better than that. Cash." He opened a drawer, extracted a manila envelope, dropped it on the desktop.

"Well, thanks. That's nice of you," Budge said. The envelope looked rather thick, which meant probably quite a bit of money, which meant what Winsor now wanted him to do was probably either dangerous or something unusually nasty. The fact it was cash certainly meant Winsor was willing to give up the tax deduction he'd get by making it salary. Therefore, Winsor wanted to leave no way it could be tracked back to Winsor.

Winsor picked up the envelope and tossed it to Budge. He let it fall onto his lap.

"What have I done to deserve this?"

"I didn't make a list," Winsor said, smiling again. "But the first thing that comes to mind is that time we had the head shyster for Amareal Corporation over here. And I let you know that I really needed to get a look at what was on those papers he was carrying in his briefcase, you remember that, and that night after you hauled the wino bastard back to his hotel, you came back with copies for me."

Budge nodded, remembering. The man had been drunk, but not as drunk as he wanted to be. When Winsor had sent Budge a scrawled note, telling him what was needed, he had remembered an all-night Kinko's copy center around the corner from a convenient bar. He'd suggested his passenger might like a nightcap, stopped at a bar, explained limo drivers have to stay with their vehicle, and, when his passenger was on the bar stool, extracted the folder from the case, hurried it into Kinko's, got the copies done, got the refilled folder back into the briefcase, and talked his tipsy passenger out of the bar, back into the limo, and turned him over to the hotel doorman.

Winsor had been waiting. "How'd you do that?"

Budge explained it.

Winsor laughed. "The son of a bitch never had a clue. Never guessed how we screwed him. And how about that time you got the Bible Belt congressman photographed with the bimbo. How'd you do that?"

Winsor already knew how that had been done. In fact, had outlined the plan himself. But Budge was patient. He explained it. With this much preparation, the next job Winsor intended to hand him must be something special. As he sat through two more examples of his under- cover deeds, his sense of dread was growing.

Finally, Winsor got to it.

"One more problem I want you to handle for me," he said. "This girl I've been having you drive here and there, she's become a serious problem."

Budge drew in his breath.

"Which one?"

"The feisty little brunette. Sorts out my lawyer paperwork, keeps it filed, thinks she's going to be a lawyer. She's copied off a bunch of very sensitive stuff. Letters, so forth. Confidential material. The little bitch wants to blackmail me with it."

"What's her name?" Budge knew the name. He wanted to make Winsor say it. He wanted a moment to think. He was sure Winsor was lying. But how could he deal with this?

"Chrissy something-or-other," Winsor said. "Some sort of Wop last name."

"Oh, yes," Budge said. "She talks a lot."

Winsor nodded. "Too damn much," he said. "I want her to disappear."

"Send her away somewhere, you mean? Different assignment at one of your companies?"

Winsor studied Budge a long moment. "You're playing dumb, aren't you? Didn't I mention blackmail? This is dead-serious business."

"So what do you want me to do?"

"I want a permanent solution to this. I want this problem eliminated. Permanently, absolutely, and eternally."

"Kill her?"

"That's part of it. But there has to be a way we can do it so it won't cause us any damage. I can help by setting her up for it."

And with that, Winsor explained what he had in mind.

Now, behind Budge in the little jet, Winsor was fastening his seat belt. They were close enough now to see the smokestacks of the old smelter. Budge eased back on the throttle and began a slow pass over the graded earth landing strip to make certain it looked safe. He noticed a large panel truck parked beside the doors of the only new-looking building on the grounds— a slope-roofed box with metal walls. The only other vehicles visible were a black sports utility vehicle parked next to the strip, with a red convertible looking tiny beside it. But nothing on the strip itself made it look riskier than landing on dirt always is.

It turned out to be a smooth one. Budge rolled the jet up to the cars, shut off the engines, and watched the three men waiting with the vehicles.

Rawley Winsor climbed out of the plane and looked at Budge. "Stay in the plane," Winsor said. "I'll either be right back, or I'll send someone for you."

Two of the men stood by the door and greeted Winsor with bows and signs of respect. The other one—wearing a Mexican army fatigue uniform and the symbols of a colonel— stood aside, studying the Falcon 10. He grinned at Budge.

"**Una** Dessault," he said, his tone full of approval. **"Una Falcona Diez?"**

"**Exactamente,**" Budge said, returning the grin. "**En Inglés, una** Falcon Ten. **Quiere usted ver la enterior?**"

The colonel's grin widened. He did, indeed, wish to see the interior. But Winsor cut off the conversation, climbed into the SUV with his greeters, and they drove off to where the truck was parked near the smelter. Budge gave them time to get there, climbed out of the jet, stretched, yawned, made sure all was secured, and followed them at an unhurried walk.

A fourth man was sitting behind the wheel of the truck. He nodded to Budge, said, "**Como esta?**"

"**Bien. Y usted?**"

The driver shrugged.

Budge walked through the doorway into the new building.

There wasn't much in it. Winsor and the two who had greeted him so warmly were clustered at an odd-looking structure mounted atop two pipes jutting from the floor. Each of these supporting legs was equipped with a wheel, which Budge guessed would open and close some sort of pressure valves. If that guess was right, he presumed those valves would control the flow of something—natural gas, air, fluids—that was being forced under pressure into the larger pipe that these two legs supported. Budge estimated the large pipe had an interior diameter of eighteen or twenty inches, and it had its own set of valve wheels. The butt end near Budge was closed with a stainless-steel screw-on cap with a plate on it that read PIG LAUNCHER, and, in smaller print, something that looked like MERICAM SPECIALTY PRODUCTS. From that terminal the pipe angled downward and disappeared out the back wall of the building.

Budge's guess about the legs—literally "pipe stem legs"—being sources of pumped pressure was quickly confirmed. Air hoses from a new-looking gasoline engine and pressure pump were connected to them. The engine running, the pump was working, and one of Winsor's greeters, clad in blue coveralls, seemed to be showing Winsor which levers opened which vents to deliver the pressurized air into the pipe.

Budge spent a moment trying to fathom what all this meant, decided he lacked any helpful knowledge, and looked around the room. The uniformed Mexican stood beside a wall, studying him. Behind the Mexican was an orderly stack of sacks, apparently of sturdy white plastic. Two other men, shirtless, wearing sandals and dusty overalls, had one of the sacks open and were spooning white stuff from one of the sacks into a cup. He weighed the cup on a scale sitting on the floor beside them and then poured it carefully into a funnel stuck in a hole in what looked to Budge like a slightly oversized soccer ball—bright yellow and seemingly equipped with a large screw-out cap. A long double row of such balls was lined against the wall. They adjoined a stack of tubes, metallic-looking but perhaps plastic. Each was about three feet long with their ends screwed on like bottle caps. Budge studied the balls and tubes, concluded they were about the size to fit inside the pipe.

For what purpose? It seemed likely to Budge that the white powder in the sack was cocaine, and the purpose was to fit the balls full of it into the pipe and use the air-pressure system to push them to wherever the pipe went. Which must be to that rich and self-indulgent North American dope market. Which must mean the pipe extended under the U.S. border and thus was invisible to the watchful scrutiny of the U.S. Border Patrol with its helicopters and drone aircraft patrols.

If that guess was right, it eliminated some of the uncertainty for Budge. That cocaine, even if it was cut with some sort of diluting powder, would be worth many, many millions. The last he'd read about the drug trade listed high-quality uncut coke at thirty thousand dollars a kilogram in New York. Maybe less now, or maybe more. With Rawley Winsor involved in this project, the stuff here was probably pure.

No wonder this project now had such high priority for Winsor. And no wonder he seemed desperate to keep the War on Drugs alive and well. Legalizing marijuana, or any of the stuff Congress liked to call "controlled substances," would eliminate the multibillion-dollar profits and quickly reduce the market size. Users would be buying in licensed government stores, with the profits and taxes going into rehabilitation programs. Even worse for the drug barons, the glamour of doing something illegal would be gone for the teenagers, and there'd be no reason left for the drug gangs to hire them to push the stuff in school yards and keep the list of customers multiplying.

Winsor was walking up, frowning.

"I told you to stay with the plane," he said.

"I did," Budge said. "Then I had to take a leak, get a little exercise, and I decided to see what was keeping you so long."

"You stepped into something that you may wish you hadn't. Sticky stuff," Winsor said. He glanced at the uniformed Mexican. So did Budge. The Mexican, looking embarrassed, glanced away.

"What's the difference," Budge said. He waved across the floor. "This is interesting. What's in the sacks? Something illegal, I'd bet. And what's with the pipe gadget there?"

Winsor glared at him. Then he shook his head. "Nothing you want to talk about," he said. "Not ever."

"If somebody ever wanted to talk about it with me, all I could say is I'm no expert but it looks to me like Rawley Winsor has something going with the Mexicans to reopen that old smelter, reopen a pipeline to bring in the fuel, and start using the equipment for something or other. Get some engineer or geologist to find out what. Maybe Mr. Winsor's going to be drilling for oil. Something like that."

Winsor was grinning. "Budge," he said. "You should know by now you can't kid me. If I believed you're as stupid as you want me to believe you wouldn't be working for me."

Budge considered that. "Fair enough," he said. "But either you trust me all the way, or you don't trust me at all, and if you don't, then I quit. But the way it is, I'm working for you. What do you want me to do now?"

"Come on," Winsor said, walking toward the door. "Let's get out of here. The colonel serves as sort of an envoy for the Mexicans invested in this business. He and I are going to get some business done. I want you back at the plane. And I want you to be remembering what happens to you if you do decide to quit."

He stopped at the door, stared at Budge.

"You understand what I'm saying?" Winsor asked.

"I do."

"We still have most of that bundle of pesos in the plane and we don't want anyone breaking in. Eat that lunch you brought. Get some sleep. We're going over the border to the Tuttle Ranch bright and early tomorrow. Landing on another dirt strip. You'll want to be fresh."

"OK," Budge said. "I'll have to call the FAA folks and make sure they know we have clearance. Do you have any problem with that."

"None," Winsor said. He handed Budge a photograph. "Nice-looking girl there. Take a good look at her."

Budge agreed. She was nice-looking. Great

eyes. Nice-shaped face. And, he noticed, nice shape even in that uniform she was wearing.

"Who is she? And why am I supposed to get interested?"

"Well, . . ." Winsor said. "Did I mention before we left that you might have to kill a cop? . . . Well, this is her. The Mexicans in this business agree she looks like a serious problem. Some sort of an undercover agent planted in the Border Patrol. They said they dealt with one such problem for us. That fellow who . . . that fellow who got himself shot in a hunting accident up in northern New Mexico. The colonel says they eliminated that problem for us and now it's our turn."

"Another Chrissy?"

"Different motives, but the same idea. And it may not be so simple for you this time. With a federal cop, you'll damn sure want to make it slick as silk. Maybe you can arrange to get her on the Falcon and dump her off into those mountains down in Mexico.

22

Budge had consumed what was left in his coffee Thermos, used some water from his jug to give his face a wakeup scrub, and was watching the dawn turn high clouds on the western horizon red, and then pink, when the SUV rolled up beside the Falcon 10 and discharged Winsor and the Mexican colonel. Budge climbed out of the plane to meet them.

"Colonel," Winsor said. "This is Mr. de Baca, my assistant. Budge de Baca. Colonel Diego de Vargas is representing our partner in this venture."

Budge said, "How do you do," and the colonel said, **"Con mucho gusto."** They eyed each other and shook hands.

"Time to go," Winsor said. "The colonel

and I want to be there to see those deliveries arriving."

"**Ah, sí,**" the colonel said, smiling broadly at the thought. **"Los puercos muy ricos."**

Winsor was grinning, too. "Yep, very rich pigs indeed," he said. "And it's been a hell of a lot of work and worry to get them safely immigrated."

Budge looked at Winsor. "You riding up front this time or with Colonel de Vargas?"

"The colonel's a pilot," Winsor said. "He'd said he'd like to fly the Falcon."

"Are we going to that game ranch in New Mexico?" Budge asked. "You like the idea of a guy landing a strange airplane the first time he's flown it, and having to put it down on a short dirt strip?"

Winsor grinned, shook his head. The colonel looked disappointed, and Budge noticed that.

"Why don't you take the copilot's seat, Colonel," Budge said, motioning him toward it. "I'll show you some of the gadgets the French built into this thing."

"Oh, good," the colonel said, smiling happily. "And people call me Diego."

As a crow flies, or a pipeline runs, the trip

from San Pedro de los Corralitos is short indeed, not much more than a hundred miles. As a Dessault Falcon 10 jet flies across the U.S. border from Mexico it's more complicated. The colonel had explained some of those complications as they buckled in and prepared for take-off, telling Budge, in Spanish, with a few technical terms mixed in, about where and when the Border Patrol flew its helicopters, where radar stations were and what they covered, and how flying too low involved a risk of encountering the pilotless drones and their cameras, which sent what they were viewing back to television screens in Border Patrol stations.

Budge took the Falcon toward El Paso, low, and far enough south to avoid radar, then gained altitude and crossed the border on a direct route toward Albuquerque until, fifty miles over New Mexico, he turned west as if headed for Tucson, explaining the little jet to Diego as he did.

The flight took time, and Budge needed time. He wanted to get acquainted with this Mexican who, he sensed, might be useful, might be subject to persuasion that killing a Border Patrol cop was not a wise idea. And he had to decide what to do about the cop herself, no matter what. And, finally, he couldn't get Chrissy off his mind.

She had brought her luggage with her that black day—that last day he'd seen her—excited, nervous, happy as she watched him fitting the bags into the limo's trunk.

"Did Rawley tell you where we're going this morning?"

"He didn't say," Budge said. "And that's very unusual. I want you to sit up front with me so we can talk about it."

"Sure," Chrissy said. "We're going out to the airport. To his airplane, and we're going to fly down to Mazatlán, down to that Mexican resort on the Pacific. And guess what?! Rawley and I are going to get married down there."

Now, flying east toward El Paso and the morning sun, he remembered every second of that day. He had closed the limo door behind her, walked around the front, got in, started the engine, and rolled down the drive to the street, trying to collect his wits. Even though he'd known this was going to happen, had been trying to form a workable plan for dealing with it, this had left him speechless—enraged, engulfed in hatred for Rawley Winsor. It hadn't occurred to him Winsor would use a ruse like this mar-riage idea. The man's cruelty amazed him.

"Aren't you excited for me?" Chrissy said. "I've never been to Mexico before. I've never even seen the Pacific Ocean."

"Chrissy. What did he tell you?"

"What do you mean?"

"I mean he must have said something about why he wasn't flying down there with you. How did he explain that? Is he flying down later? Do I go back and get him? He'd told me he wants me ready to fly him down to El Paso, or maybe somewhere in New Mexico, and all on very short notice. What's the plan here?"

"Budge. What's wrong? You sound funny?"

He stopped for a red light, signaled a turn. How could he tell her what Winsor planned for her? How could he tell her so she would believe him. She would think he was jealous. Lying. He couldn't just abduct her with force. If he did, what then. And if he told her, and she didn't be-lieve him, she'd call Winsor. And Winsor would pretend to believe her, assure her that Budge was just crazy jealous. Then Winsor would get him out of the picture and dispose of Chrissy another way. He'd have to find a way to show her the truth.

"Did Mr. Winsor tell you when he was coming down? Do you have a date for the wedding? Any of that?"

"He had a job he had to finish. Just another day he thought. He said you'd be bringing him down tomorrow." She paused. "But I guess you already knew that. He must have mentioned it to you. Didn't he?" Chrissy's tone had wavered from angry to uncertain.

"Tomorrow? That's not possible unless he changes his other plans. Are you sure?"

"Of course I'm sure," she said. But now she didn't sound sure. She sounded shaken.

"Is someone meeting you when we get to Mazatlán? At the airport. Maybe a hotel limo service? Which hotel?"

"He didn't tell you that?" She reached into her purse, extracted a card, read from it: "Hotel la Maya, 172 Calle Obregon, Mazatlán."

She stared at him. "I guess I go down there and check in, and when Rawley arrives tomorrow I'll ask him when he gets there. But what do I ask him? Ask him why he forgot to tell you about this? You could ask him yourself when you're flying him on the way down."

He sighed. Said: "Chrissy—" But he cut it

off. Her tone was stiff again. She didn't want to know. He'd have to show her.

He'd expected to find that Winsor had not bothered to make a reservation at Hotel la Maya, and to use that solid, concrete evidence to add some credibility to what he had to say. Then he would explain that Winsor hadn't expected her to reach Mazatlán, that Winsor had told him that she was blackmailing him, that she had copied confidential materials from his legal files, that she had evolved an extortion plot, and that he had ordered Budge to dispose of her. He imagined Chrissy hysterical, demanding to know why he was lying to her. He imagined her rushing to a telephone to call Winsor. What could he do to stop her? And what would happen next?

Winsor, however, proved to have been overconfident.

Chrissy sat in the passenger seat behind him on the flight down, silent. No hotel limo was awaiting them. He took the cab with her from the airport to the hotel, told the cabbie to wait, and surrendered her bags at the entry to the greeter.

"I'll take care of things from here, Budge,"

she said. "It was nice of you to worry about me, but go home now."

"I'll make sure your reservations are correct," Budge said, and followed her in.

Of course they weren't.

The desk clerk's English was perfect. He looked puzzled. "We seem to have a mistake," he said. "Some confusion, I think. Was there a second reservation? A Mr. Rawley Winsor, of Washington, D.C., often keeps a suite here and I believe he is here now." He glanced down at his record again. "No, Mrs. Winsor is in occupation. She arrived last week. According to this, she will stay here until next Tuesday, I believe."

"He reached for the telephone. "I will call Mrs. Winsor. Was she expecting you to join her?"

Budge glanced at Chrissy standing motionless and speechless beside him. She looked faint. He took her arm.

"No," he said. "We've made a mistake."

He recovered her luggage, ushered her out to the cab, and told the driver to take them to the airport. En route, he told her everything, how Winsor had ordered him to kill her and dispose of the body. She listened, wordless.

"That's all of it," he said, and noticed she

was shaking. "Now, ask me any questions, and if you don't have any, just tell me what you want to do."

"I wonder why you are telling me all this."

"Because it's true, Chrissy," he said. "And because no one should be treated like this. Certainly nobody like you. Do you believe me."

"I don't know. Some of it, I guess. Maybe a lot of it."

He thought a moment. "Remember that day you showed me that ring? His grandmother's ring he told you, with the huge diamond. Do you have it with you?"

"No," she said.

"Where is it?"

"Do you want it?"

"No, Chrissy. I don't want it. But why don't you have your engagement ring with you? Why aren't you wearing it."

"He asked for it back. So he could have the jeweler clean it and fit it to my finger size."

"When?"

"Tuesday afternoon."

"It was Wednesday morning he told me to get rid of you. To dispose of you. Permanently."

"Why are you—" She cut off the question,

shuddered, and said, "Oh," in something like a whisper.

He put his arm around her shoulders and hugged her to him. "In a little while we'll be at the airport. I don't want to take you back to your apartment because if you go there, he will hear about it. He'll know I didn't follow my orders. He'll still think you're dangerous to him. I'm not sure you'd be safe there. But what do you want to do?"

"I don't care," Chrissy said, still in a whisper.

"If you still have some doubts about me, do you want to find a room here, and wait, and see if he comes to the Hotel la Maya?"

"No. No. No. Not that."

"You could come home with me. Stay at my place. And call the Maya tomorrow to find out if he comes."

"No."

"Not stay at my place?"

"Not call. I would never call about that. But I think I would stay down here for a little while. I feel tired. And sort of sick. Could we find another hotel where I could stay a day or two?"

They did, and checked her in, and he took the cab back to the airport. Budge was remembering that return flight now. His relief, the feel-

ing of the tension draining out him, a sort of ju-
bilation. But the happy thought was interrupted.
The colonel's voice intruded in Spanish:

"You handled that very nicely," Diego said.

"What?"

"The turbulence back there. Neatly done.
Where did you learn to fly? From your Spanish,
I thought perhaps it would have been in Cuba."

"Some of it was," Budge said. "And you,
Diego. Where did you learn the trade?"

"Some in Mexico. And later on, some in El
Salvador." He chuckled. "For that very generous
Central Intelligence Agency, courtesy of the
United States taxpayers. And some in Panama,
when their **presidente** was the drug boss down
there." Diego laughed. "He was also on the CIA
payroll at the time, but they were paying him a
lot more than I got. Your boss told me we have
that CIA experience in common."

"Well, I flew some for the CIA."

"Yes," Diego de Vargas said. "Not very pleasant to work for. Nor reliable." He chuckled. "I
can say the same thing for my own present patron. **Muy rico.** And very, very willing to kill
somebody if they seem inconvenient. Including
me, I have no doubt."

"He and my patron seem perfectly matched

in this business," Budge said. "Why did he have that man killed up in northern New Mexico? That seems a long way from this."

Diego turned his head, glanced back at Winsor in the seat behind him, then looked at Budge.

"You're dead certain he doesn't understand Spanish?"

"His second language is bad French," Budge said. "He once heard me talking to one of his Mexican cleaning ladies and said something about not wanting any of his friends to hear that low-down language in his house."

"Low-down? He meant undignified?"

"Trashy," Budge said. "Low class. He won't understand you. So tell me why that man was killed way up there."

"I think it was a mistake. He was asking a lot of questions about pipelines. And about products being shipped through the wrong ones. The chief thought he should be erased and they decided the Mexican end of their project should handle it."

"How about your uniform?"

"I'm a former colonel. But now it's more or less honorary. The Reform Party won the election, and the good old PIRG is out, and

President Fox is in. The PIRG people are getting fired, especially in the police and the military. These days I get paid through some big shot in Banco de Mexico, and I think he takes his orders from somebody in the Colombian cartel, and I don't think that's going to last very long. I hear the Fox people are after him, too."

Diego sighed, shook his head. "My boss, he's a miserable bastard. But I hear even worse stuff about your chief."

"Believe it."

"I heard he is so connected he could get you deported by just saying the word," Diego said. "I heard they'd like to lock you up in Guatemala. If your patron speaks to the right people they haul you off to jail." Diego shook his head. "I've seen those Guatemala lockups, man. You want to avoid that experience."

Budge didn't respond. He adjusted something on the instrument panel.

"You never know about gossip," Diego said. "They say bad things about me, too." He shrugged. "Some of them are true. How about you?"

"Well, I know my patron could give me some serious trouble if he wanted to do it."

"Maybe he's doing that right now," Diego

said. "Getting us in serious trouble, I mean. He says that woman who has been snooping around here is probably in the Border Patrol just to find out what we're doing. I mean the one in the picture they've been handing around. I think the plan is to have her killed."

Budge made another slight flight instrument adjustment, thought a moment, made a decision.

"Diego, I'm going to get very serious now. And tell you some things. The first is, I think you're right. The second is, you and I are going to be lucky if we get out of this situation like free men, alive and well. And the third is, if that woman gets killed by anybody, we're going to be the ones hanged for it. Just us. Not anybody who told us to do it."

Diego sat silent for a long moment. And when he spoke his voice was very low. "What are you telling me?"

"That man sitting behind us, he thinks he has had this all arranged to perfection. His cocaine comes flowing through the pipe from Mexico. No more Border Patrol problems. It gets unloaded very simply, goes from his ranch here right into Phoenix, and then into the big-city markets, pure profits. A flawless plan. Absolutely no way anything could possibly go wrong. But you and I, we have already seen it hasn't been flawless."

"You mean the man killed up north. That's true. We hear now that was a mistake. I don't like mistakes."

"Especially, I don't like mistakes that might get me in prison. Or get me killed."

Diego stared straight ahead, thinking. Then he glanced at Budge, his expression wry.

"You've been in the U.S. of A. a long time. The patron"—he nodded toward Winsor behind him—"he seems to think you can kill this woman cop and get away with it. What do you think about that."

"I don't know what he thinks. But I think that if we kill her, he has it figured out so he'll get away with it. But if he has it figured right, she is a federal cop. The federals will catch us, wherever we go. Not give up until they do. And then they either kill us or we die in a federal prison somewhere. And, of course, that's exactly the way the chief hopes it will work out. He wouldn't want us around anymore."

Diego sighed. "Yes," he said. "It would be

true also among those where I've always
worked."

"The way it happens in Washington, my patron is rich and powerful, and his roomful of
lawyers and very important friends let the police
know that our rich and powerful boss is innocent. He just came out here to shoot an African
antelope for his trophy room. And he had me
put his special trophy hunting rifle back there in
the storage place to show them evidence that
that's the truth. And then he says he was be-
trayed by two low-class scoundrels who already
are wanted by the police."

"Yes," he said. "That sounds like it would be
in Mexico too."

"I think there is a way out of this for us,"
Budge said.

"Tell me," Diego said.

Winsor's voice intruded:

"Hey, Budge," Winsor said. "There's the
ranch up there ahead. You guys knock off that
Mex gabbing and pay attention to business. You
think that strip looks safe enough?"

"I'll lose some altitude and circle," Budge
said. "Why take chances." He flew over the
Tuttle Ranch headquarters, the big tile-roofed
ranch house, and the row of mobile homes

where the hired hands lived, the barns, the stables, the horse pasture, the stock tank with its connected windmill. He studied the landing strip. It was a straight and narrow black band pointing into the prevailing winds. It looked blacker than he remembered, apparently recently stabilized by a fresh coating of oil. The windsock on the pole atop the little hanger reported a mild westerly breeze was blowing. He was low enough to see the nose of the ranch's little Piper backed into the hanger and to recognize that the dark blue sports utility vehicle parked beside it was a Land Rover.

He turned to look at Winsor. "See anything there you don't want to see?"

"No. How about you?"

"Looked good," Budge said, and banked again, completing the circle, leveling off toward the southwest into the landing approach position.

"When we get on the ground, you can leave most of that luggage stowed away. We won't be here more than a few hours. But I want you to get out that pet rifle of mine, and the gear that goes with it. We'll take that along when we go out to the pig trap."

"Pig trap?"

"Pipeliner lingo," Winsor said. "The pig's what they call the thing they push down through the pipeline to clean it out, or find leaks, so forth. That gadget you saw on the pipeline at the old smelter, that's where they put the pig into the pipeline. It's the pig launcher. When they get the pig where it's going, they divert it out of the line into a pig trap."

"Now you're going to tell me why you're taking your rifle to the pig trap," Budge said.

"Going to shoot me a scimitar-horned oryx for my trophy room," Winsor said. "And maybe I'll also help you with that job I assigned to you."

"Killing the cop?" Budge asked. "That woman in the picture? How are we going to find her?"

Winsor laughed. "That's all arranged," he said. "Her duty this morning is to drive out to the back gate of the Tuttle Ranch and go take another look at that construction site where she took all those photographs."

"Oh," Budge said. He felt sick. Stunned. He'd underestimated Winsor again. He'd thought there was no practical way he'd be expected to find that woman, and he'd dreamed up the scenario he'd been giving to Diego in the hope of forming some sort of alliance if he needed one. He'd thought Winsor was simply exercising his macho bravado. That this problem would go away. But Winsor had found a way to make the nightmare become real.

"When you're working for me, Budge, you don't leave things to chance. You arrange things. Like I had them put a big old tarp in the back of the Land Rover. Big enough to keep a trophy-sized oryx head from bleeding all over the upholstery. Plenty big to hold that little cop until we fly her back over the Mexican mountains and drop her off."

23

Sergeant Jim Chee had no trouble awakening before dawn in the motel at Lordsburg. He had hardly slept. He couldn't guide his self-conscious into any of those calm, relaxing reveries that bring on sleep. Instead he listened to Cowboy Dashee, comfortable in the adjoining bed, mixing his snoring with an occasional unfinished, undecipherable sleep-talker statement. Some of it was in English, but since he never finished a sentence, or even a phrase, that was as incomprehensible to Chee as when his muttering was in Hopi.

Before five A.M. they were dressed, checked out, and down at a truck stop beside Interstate 10. Cowboy ordered pancakes, sausage, and coffee. So did Chee. But he didn't feel like eating. Cowboy did, and between bites, studied Chee.

"What's the trouble?" he asked. "Worried, or is it love sick?"

"Worried," Chee said. "How am I going to get Bernie to quit this damned Border Patrol job and come on home?"

"That's easy," Cowboy said.

"Like hell," Chee said. "You just don't understand how stubborn she is."

"That's not my problem, ole buddy. What I don't understand is how you can stay so stupid so long."

"Don't talk with your mouth full of pancake," Chee said.

"If you want her to come home, you just say, 'Bernie, my sweet, I love you dearly. Come home and marry me and we will live happily ever after.'"

"Yeah," Chee said.

"Maybe you'd also have to tell her you'd get rid of that junky old trailer home of yours down by the river, and live in a regular house. Decent insulation, running water, regular beds instead of bunks, all that."

"Come on, Cowboy. Be serious. I ask Bernie to marry me. She says, 'Why would I want to do that?' Then what do I say?"

"You tell her, 'Because I love you, and you

love me, and when that happens, people get married.'"

"Dream on," Chee said, and followed that with a dismissive snort and a brooding silence. Then: "You think so?"

"What?"

"That she likes me?"

"Damn it, Jim, she loves you."

"I don't think so. I wouldn't bet she even likes me."

"Find out," Cowboy said. "Ask her."

Chee sighed. Shook his head.

"What's the trouble?"

"Cowardice, I guess," Chee said.

"Afraid she'll hurt your feelings?"

"You know my record," Chee said.

"You mean Janet Pete?" Cowboy said. "The way I read that affair, I figured you dumped her instead of vice versa."

"It wasn't that simple," Chee said. "But start with Mary Landon. Remember her. Beautiful blue-eyed blonde teacher at Crownpoint Middle School, and I wanted to marry her, and she liked the idea but she let me know that what she wanted was somebody to take back to her family's big dairy farm in Wisconsin, and I'd be the male she rescued from the savages."

"I didn't know her," Cowboy said. "I think that was before I disobeyed my family and friends and started associating with you Navajos."

"You'd have loved her," Chee said. "I sure thought I did, and it really hurt when I finally understood the feeling wasn't mutual."

"How about Janet? I still see her in federal court now and then when her Washington office sends her out on a case. A real classy lady."

"Different version of the same story," Chee said. "I was all set to propose to Janet. In fact, I sort of thought I had. Borrowed a videotape a fellow had made of his daughter's traditional marriage, all that. But it turned out Janet was the perfect model of what the sociologists call assimilation. Dad a city Navajo. Mother a super-sophisticated, high-society Washingtonian socialite. Janet was all set to take me back as her trophy sheep camp Navajo. She had a socially acceptable job picked out for me. The whole package. She didn't want Jim Chee. She wanted what she thought she could turn him into."

Through this discourse, Cowboy was finishing his sausage and looking thoughtful. "Twice burned, you're thinking. So triple cautious. But the Bernie I know, and the one you tell me about, is a bona fide Navajo. She's not going to want to drag you off somewhere to try to civilize you."

"I know," Chee said. "I've just got a feeling that if I make a move on her, she'll just tell me she's not interested."

Cowboy stared at him. Shook his head. "Well, I guess there's lots of reasons she'd kiss you off. Total lack of romantic instincts, for example. Or maybe she's spotted an abnormal level of stupidity and decided it's incurable. I'm beginning to see that problem myself."

With that Cowboy signaled for the waitress, reminded Chee the expenses on this trip were his responsibility, and handed him the breakfast bill.

"Well, anyway, let's get on down to the Tuttle Ranch and take a look at that sinister construction project of theirs. Come on, Cowboy," he said. "Eat. Choke it down, or wash it down with your coffee, or bring it along. Let's go."

Dashee grumbled but they went, and thus by the time the sun was rising over the Cedar Mountain range to the east, and turning the flat little cloud cap over Hat Top Mountain a glorious pink, they were exiting County Road 146, slowing a little for the sleeping village of

Hachita, and creating clouds of dust along the gravel of County Road 81 down the great emptiness of the Hachita Valley.

"You sure you know where we're going?" Cowboy asked.

"Yes," Chee said, and he did. But he wasn't exactly sure how to get there. And Dashee sensed that.

"That map you have there on your lap. Aren't those the Big Hatchet Mountains over there to our left?"

"Um, yee-aaow, it looks like they ought to be," Chee said, very slowly and reluctantly.

"Then from what you told me about where that Tuttle Ranch south gate is located, we seem to have missed a turn somewhere. Seems we might be going in the wrong direction."

"Looks like it."

"Then let's stop the next place we get to and ask directions," Dashee suggested.

"The next place we get to is Antelope Wells. That's the port of entry on the Mexican border, and it's about fifty miles south of here, and the last twenty or so, according to this map, are marked unimproved."

Dashee pulled his BLM truck off the road,

parked it among the scattered creosote bushes, and got out.

"Here's my plan," he said. "We turn around and head back toward where we came from. You do the driving and I'll do the navigating. Give me your map. It is well known among us Hopis, and all other tribes, that Navajos aren't to be relied upon when it comes to understanding maps."

And so it happened, that it was late morning when Chee finally yelled, "Yes, this is it. I remember driving right past that bunch of mesquite over there. And that soaptree yucca. Take that little right turn there, and up that set of tracks, and up that hill, and from there we can see the Tuttle Ranch south gate."

"Well, good," Dashee said. "Getting there on Navajo Time, we other Indians say, means late. But better late than never."

At the top of the hill they could indeed see the gate, and it was open.

"Maybe I wouldn't have needed you," Chee said. "I could have driven right in."

"No, you'd still be lost. And you'd be asked for your jurisdiction credentials right away, and tossed right out again."

"Anyway, through the gate and over two hills and then we're there," Chee said. "I measured it on my odometer. A fraction less than four miles to go."

It proved to be 3.7 miles from the gate to the hilltop from which they could see the construction site. And the new building. A dark green Border Patrol pickup was parked behind it.

Chee said: "Son of a bitch!"

Dashee gave Chee a wry look.

"Is that what she drives?" he asked. "You think Bernie's there?"

"I hope not," Chee said. She must be crazy. Why in God's name would she come out here again. She knows the dopers have her picture. She knows they think she's dangerous."

"Let's talk about that later," Dashee said. "Now let's get right on down there. Let's hope this case of being late is going to be one of those better-than-never times."

Dashee pulled the car back onto the track in a flurry of dirt-throwing wheel spinning and headed it down the hill.

24

That morning, Customs Patrol Officer Bernadette Manuelito had pulled her Border Patrol vehicle onto the dusty shoulder of Playas Road, stepped out, taken her jish out of her purse, extracted a little prescription bottle from it, and shook a pinch of corn pollen onto her left palm. She stood a moment, staring eastward toward the Big Hatchet Mountains. A streak of cloud hanging atop the mountain ridge was turned a brilliant yellow by the rising sun, then orange that faded into red. CPO Manuelito sang the chant greeting the sun. She blessed the dawning new day with a sprinkle of pollen and climbed back into the car.

Her prayer this morning, she was thinking, was a bit more fervent than usual. She had set her alarm for five A.M. and left her home in

Rodeo very quietly, not wanting to awaken Eleanda, whose regular breathing she could hear in the adjoining bedroom. Ed Henry's call had come last night just after she'd watched the weather report on the evening news and hit the sack.

The TV weatherman had sent along some hope that maybe tomorrow would be a rainout, and if the Border Patrol actually had such holidays she would certainly enjoy one. Yesterday had been long, tiring, and unproductive, spent with two other CPOs, both male and both experienced, following the tracks of ten or eleven people, presumed to be illegals, northward through the San Bernadino Valley in extreme southeastern Arizona into the edge of the Chiricahuc Mountains.

The afternoon had been hot, with a gusty wind blowing dust up her pant legs and stinging her face. The other officers, a Tohono O'odham local and a White Mountain Apache, had assumed the role of her teachers. They had laughed off her experience as a Navajo police officer and cast her as a green recruit who was probably teachable, but incurably a "girl." They had explained why the group they were tracking were not merely illegals slipping into the U.S. in search of minimum-wage jobs but were mules carrying illegal products. They drew her attention to the short steps being taken—evidence of carrying heavy loads—and places where these loads were put down presumably when the mules needed rest, and how some of the loads had been the sort of sacks in which marijuana is often carried. Early on Bernie had pointed to the dents in the dirt that might have been caused by luggage, or a frying pan, or some equally logical cooking utensil, but after this had produced only amused looks, she had kept her opinions to herself.

It had been almost sundown before the tracks disappeared beyond hope of retrieval, erased by the increasing wind. The two males, in charge due to seniority—and their own ideas about gender—had decided that they could think of no reason dope importers would be climbing into these empty and roadless mountains. They decided everyone should go home for the evening and tomorrow they would all continue her education by tracking down four pack horses reported to have been seen in Guadalupe Canyon in the Guadalupe Mountains.

Thus Bernie had reached Rodeo exhausted,

dusty, dehydrated, and disgruntled. Eleanda had saved some yogurt and a fruit salad for her, and they'd watched the evening news for a while. Bernie had taken her shower, climbed into pajamas and into bed. There she tried not to think of tomorrow's chore, tried to remember why she had thought joining the Border Control Shadow Wolves unit was such a good idea, and finally comforted herself with a couple of her happier memories of Sergeant Jim Chee. She was just getting sleepy, and was hoping that the weatherman knew what he was talking about, that the already late monsoons might be starting tomorrow, and if it did rain, she wouldn't be hunting pack horses in a mountain canyon.

That's when the telephone rang.

"It's for you," Eleanda shouted. "The boss."

Ed Henry, as always, was short and to the point. "Got a schedule change for you tomorrow," he said. "Cancel that tracking job over in the Guadalupes. They're predicting rain anyway. I want you to go out to that construction site on the Tuttle Ranch. Get there bright and early. Look around. See what's happening and let me know."

"You mean back to that gate? Do you think they'll let me in this time?"

"They know now it was just a mistake when you followed that truck in there. You didn't do no harm."

Bernie spent a moment dealing with her surprise. Then she said a doubtful sounding "OK," and asked Henry what he was expecting to find. "Am I supposed to be looking for something specific?"

"Bernie," he said, "I sort of owe you an apology. I've been thinking about everything you told me, and it seemed to me that maybe something not quite right might be going on out there. So just go out and take another look around, and give me a call and let me know what you think."

"Fine."

"And use that cell phone number I gave you. I got some running around to do tomorrow so I won't be in the office. In fact, I'll be coming out to the Tuttle place myself later in the day. I'll sort of serve as your backup." With that, Henry chuckled.

Now, back on the road again with the morning sunlight flooding the valley and clouds beginning to build up over mountains in every direction, Bernie was remembering that chuckle instead of enjoying the vast expanse of beauty. Would it finally rain? That was no longer among the questions on her mind. What kind of thinking had Ed Henry been doing to cause him to reconsider the Tuttle Ranch? What did he think she might find? Why did Henry think the gate would be unlocked this time? That must be because he'd arranged for someone to let her in. Or to let him in. He'd said he was coming out himself a little later. That thought reminded her of the picture Henry had taken of her, and what Delos Vasquez had told her about seeing a copy of it held by one of the drug gangs in Mexico.

By the time she reached the hilltop from which she had first looked down upon the gate, she was feeling thoroughly uneasy about this assignment. She unsnapped the strap on her holster, took out her Border Patrol pistol, and confirmed that the magazine was filled with the official number of nine-millimeter rounds of ammunition. She had scored expert at the firing range test she'd taken after applying for this job, just as she'd scored expert on the range with the similar pistol used by the Navajo Tribal Police. But she'd been shooting at targets. She'd never shot at anything alive. Certainly not at a fellow human. Could she if she had to? Maybe, she thought. Probably she could do it. She checked the safety, put the pistol back in the holster, took her binoculars out of their case, and got out of the truck.

The gate was not only unlocked, it was standing open. No vehicles anywhere around it, none in sight in any direction. No humans either, no horses, and no oryx. She focused again on the gate. Wide open. Beckoning her. She found herself wishing to see Mr. O'day driving up, wishing he would tell her she absolutely could not come in without a personal invitation from the owner and he didn't give a damn what her supervisor had told her. She gave Mr. O'day a few seconds to arrive at the gate. He didn't. She climbed back into her vehicle, rolled it down the hill through the gate, and drove slowly up the hill beyond it, and over it to the top of the next hill. There she stopped again and looked at the construction site below. No sign of motion. She got out the binoculars, stood beside the car, and studied the place.

No vehicles there, either. The construction crew was gone but it was obvious it hadn't been idle. The major change was the addition of a rectangular building, apparently a modified form of a mobile home. The small windmill that had been laying on the ground in sections on her first visit was now mounted atop the building, its blades turning slowly in the mild breeze. She scanned the surroundings carefully, changing the binocular's focus as the circle widened. Off to her left she caught motion. Focused again. Four oryx, running down the slope into the playa, where, from what she'd been told, they found water. All the animals seemed to be either immatures or females. At least none was carrying that great curved horn, the declaration of male oryx machismo, like the one she'd photographed. No horn. No other sign of life. She drove down the trail to the construction site.

No apparent reason to worry. No apparent reason for Ed Henry to send her here. Despite that, she pulled her vehicle up beside the new building where it was partially concealed. When she got out to explore, she made sure her pistol was safely in its holster.

The front door that had been installed on the building was of heavy hardwood and secured by a substantial lock. Except for that, there wasn't much remarkable about the building. It had been placed on a concrete foundation and the front and side windows covered with plywood panels. Bernie walked around behind it, looking for a back door. It had been boarded over too, but high windows on both sides of the door were still glassed. Bernie considered this, decided the need for security had been partly offset by the need to allow some fresh air and daylight to reach the interior. The slope of the land made the windows high enough to prove some safety from intruders.

She drove through the weeds and gravel to the back door and then parked with the front bumper as close as she could get it to the wall under a window. She climbed on the hood, clutched the window ledge, pulled herself up, and looked in. By the time her eyes had adjusted to the darkness inside her hands were aching from the strain, but she could see the building was a single room, mostly unfurnished. She lowered herself, rubbed her hands and wrists, kept her eyes tightly closed, and hoisted herself again.

The center of the room was occupied by an odd-looking structure made of pipes, some very large, others smaller. The purpose of this contraption seemed to Bernie to be support of a central pipe, which curved upward from the floor and terminated at a large diameter cap—reminding her of the screw-on cap of a huge peanut butter jar. This biggest pipe, and several smaller ones, were equipped with valves, perhaps to open or close them, and she could see faces of several dials. For what? She was considering that and thinking of the pain in her fingers and wrists when she heard a voice behind her.

A man's voice. It said: "Young woman. What are you looking for?" And this was followed by a laugh.

Bernie, still clinging to the windowsill, looked over her shoulder. She saw a stocky man wearing a tan hat, sunglasses, an expensive-looking hunting jacket, and boots standing behind her car, looking up at her. He held a rifle with telescopic sight cradled on his arm and sort of pointing in her direction. Behind him and to the side stood two other men. One, still wearing a neatly trimmed mustache and the military fatigues in which she had first seen him, was the Mexican driver of the Seamless Weld truck. The other was bigger, taller, short-cut reddish hair, and a dark blue shirt, and was staring at her. And when their eyes met he smiled. It seemed somehow sympathetic.

The stocky man wearing the sunglasses gestured at her with the rifle barrel.

"Get on down from there now," Sunglasses said. "If you're looking for something, come on in the shed with us and we'll show it to you."

"I'm coming," Bernie said. "Who are you? Are you Mr. Tuttle?" She lowered herself to the truck hood, jumped off in the direction away from the rifle, unsnapped her holster, saw the rifle barrel was now pointed exactly at her, and let her hand fall to her side.

"Good thinking," the man said. "Diego," he shouted, "get over here and help this young lady with her pistol."

Bernie was certain now. He was the man with the Seamless Weld truck she had followed here. He walked around the car, lifted the pistol out of her holster, said, "Sorry, madam," examined the pistol, and stuck it in his hip pocket.

"This is Mr. Diego de Vargas," Sunglasses said, "and this man over here is Budge C. de Baca." He laughed. "That 'C. de Baca' means 'Head of a Cow.'" And I am the owner of Jacob Tuttle, which makes me owner of this ranch, which puts you in distinguished company. But we want to know what you are doing here, trespassing on my property. So we'll all go inside and talk about it. Bring her along, Budge."

"You're the ranch owner?" Bernie asked. "I'd been hoping to meet you. I wanted to ask you about Mexican trucks coming in here."

"He's Rawley Winsor," Budge said, and motioned her forward. At the front of the structure, Winsor took off his sunglasses, unlocked the door, and gestured for them to follow him inside. Budge leaned against Bernie, whispered something. Bernie said, "What?"

"Do you understand Spanish?"

"Yes," she said. This wasn't what she'd expected. Wasn't what she'd been dreading. Or maybe it was.

"Tell him you're with the DEA," Budge whispered. "Tell him you can be bought."

Bernie nodded.

Winsor dusted off a wooden chair, sat himself on it.

"Set her down on the bench by the table," Winsor said. "We need to ask her some questions." He glanced at his wristwatch. "And we cut this awful short. Diego, get that trap set. It's just about time for our precious pigs to begin arriving."

De Vargas was standing beside the pipe contraption in the middle of the room. He spun a valve, causing a hissing sound, spun another.

The sound this time was more like a sigh. He seized the handles on the round cap that closed the end of the master pipe, strained, turned it, and then spun it off. Bernie smelled a rush of stale air, and then de Vargas lifted what might have been a soccer ball from the pipe. It was a dirty yellow with two thick black rubber strips around it. Gaskets, perhaps, to make it fit tightly inside the pipe. Diego put the ball on the table behind Bernie, reclosed the pipe valve, and wiped his hands on the legs of his pants.

Winsor made an impatient gesture with his hands, said: "Get the cap off."

Diego unscrewed a round cap, dropped it on the table, reached into the hole, began extracting transparent plastic sacks. He lined them on the tabletop, reached back, and brought out more. "I see they sacked it," he said.

"That'd be enough for now," Winsor said, and looked at Bernie.

"You're Officer Bernadette Manuelito, now of the Customs Service Border Patrol. Used to be Navajo Tribal Police. But we don't know why you made the switch. Explain that."

"I don't know myself," Bernie said.

Winsor decided to let that drop. He pointed to the sacks beside her.

"Do you know what that is?"

Bernie cleared her throat, glanced at Budge. He was staring at her, frowning, looking tense.

"If I had to guess I'd say those little packages contain what we like to call one of the 'uncontrollable substances.' And since it's a white powder, I'd guess it's cocaine. If it's good refined nose candy, uncut by cake sugar and the other stuff you mix it with, it should bring you something like twenty-five thousand dollars a kilo."

Winsor showed no reaction to that.

"So what are your intentions?" he asked.

"Are you asking what is my duty, or what do I intend to do? My duty is to get my pistol back from that man over there and put you all under arrest for possession of an illegal substance. However, my intention is to try to calculate how many kilos you have there, and how many more of those yellow balls you have stored in that crazy-looking pipe, and multiply all those kilos by twenty-five thousand dollars, and then multiply that by ten percent. Then I will tell you that's what my fee would be, just ten percent, for reporting to my superior that there was nothing in this shack but old furniture and rusty junk pipeline stuff."

Winsor waved Diego out of the folding chair

in which he had been sitting, moved it over in front of where Bernie sat on the table, and seated himself.

"Who is your superior? Name and position."

Bernie managed a smile. "If you're thinking of my Customs Patrol Officer uniform, thinking of the Border Patrol, then the name is Ed Henry, and he is supervisor of the unit I was loaned to, to do some checking into things— such as this. But if you're thinking of my actual boss, my superior in the Drug Enforcement Agency, I don't intend to tell you until we have some sort of arrangement."

Winsor digested this a moment. Said: "Why not?"

She shook her head. "Hate to say this but I'm not sure either one of us could trust him. Henry either, for that matter."

Winsor took a silver cigarette case from his jacket pocket, opened it, and leaned forward to offer one to Bernie, who shook her head.

He held out the case to Budge, then withdrew it, laughing. "Budge doesn't smoke, either, but I keep trying to tempt him," Winsor said. "He wants to live forever." He took one himself, snapped on the lighter built into the case, inhaled deeply, and blew out a cloud of smoke.

"What do you think of what this young lady says, Budge? Does it make sense to you?"

Budge had been watching Diego, who had been watching Winsor, expecting to be offered a cigarette. When he wasn't, his expression hardened.

"Sounds sensible," Budge said.

"Why?"

"Because ninety percent is better than a hundred, if you have to go to prison to keep the hundred."

Winsor stared at him. "I think you're forgetting that assignment I gave you."

The pig trap where Diego was standing began whistling. "What's that?" Budge said, and got up from his chair.

"It's the pig signal on top of the pipe there," Diego said. "The pressure sets it off. It tells you another pig has arrived in the trap."

"I've got to see how that works," Budge said. He pressed in against Diego, who was turning the handle on a pipe marked "BLOWDOWN VALVE." The whistling died away. Budge slipped the pistol from Diego's pocket, felt Diego's body stiffen, said, **"Bueno, bueno,** calm yourself," into Diego's ear. "Remember, we go together."

He slid the pistol under his belt, hidden by his jacket flap.

"What are you doing?" Winsor asked.

"I guess we have another of our sinister pigs arriving," Diego said.

"Budge turned to Winsor. "You want it taken out?"

"They'll be coming along regularly now," Winsor said. "Let Diego do it. I want to know if you're ready to handle your job."

"Just about," Budge said.

"I don't like the way your mind's started working. All this hesitation. Is it because this is such a good-looking young lady? Maybe your macho brainlobe is heating up. If we let this woman out of here, even if she's totally bought and paid for, how the hell can you ever rest easy again."

After saying that, Winsor shifted in the chair. The rifle resting on his lap shifted with him, its barrel turned now toward where Budge stood, leaning against the table. "We turn her loose, then she's just one more damned thing out of control. We buy her, how long does she stay bought?"

Bernie, who had been watching Budge as he

walked back from the pig trap, had shifted her attention to Winsor. She sat now, pale and silent, with her eyes half closed.

"She's a federal officer," Budge said. "From what she told you, she must have been assigned to us, more or less. If we kill her, it's going to be a top-priority case for the FBI and the DEA and everybody else. They'll never stop coming after us until they get us."

Winsor chuckled, shook his head. "Budge, there's a lot of things you just don't understand. The cops at the bottom do what the people on top tell them to do. You heard about that man shot up on the Navajo Reservation. Did I tell you that he became officially the unfortunate victim of a hunting accident." Winsor was grinning. "I guess it was a hunting accident, in a way. The Mexicans shot him because they thought he was hunting this pipeline project of ours. Now our friends in Washington tell us he was actually trying to find out who's been stealing all that Indian oil royalty money."

"If you're thinking of making Miss Manuelito a hunting accident it won't work. She doesn't look much like an oryx."

Winsor's face was flushed. "Knock it off, Budge," he said. "We're thinking of doing it just like you did Chrissy. Except you don't have the chloroform this time, and you'll drop her body out over the mountains instead of the ocean."

Budge stared at Winsor, saying nothing, thinking of Chrissy, aware that Winsor was studying him, knowing what he would have to do, knowing it was absolutely inevitable.

"Well," Winsor said, "let's get with it. He turned toward Diego. "Diego. Bring me Officer Manuelito's pistol."

Diego looked rattled. "Ah, well, I don't have it no more."

"Where the hell is it then," Winsor said. "We're going to need it. Shoot her with it. Make it look like another accident. A woman who didn't know how to handle a—"

Winsor's mouth remained open, but a sudden, and apparently terrible, thought stopped the words. He jerked his head around. Stared at Budge. Shouted: "Son of a bitch!"

What was happening was a blur of action. Winsor was swiveling in his chair, snarling an obscenity, cocking the rifle, swinging the barrel toward Budge. Budge was snatching Bernie's pistol from his belt, his expression saying that he knew he'd waited a fatal second too long.

Bernie screamed something that might have

been "No!" and kicked frantically at Winsor's rifle.

Winsor, still cursing, slammed the rifle barrel against her head, and then back at Budge as he pulled the trigger.

But now it was Winsor who was a fatal split second late.

25

Dashee's racetrack-braking technique sent his pickup into a sideways slide and produced a fountain of dust over Bernie's vehicle and the adjoining building.

"She's in the car," Chee said. "I can see the back of her head." He was out of Dashee's truck before it stopped, pulling on the handle of Bernie's car door, shouting at her. She unlocked the door, looked up at him. One of those white medical-kit bandages was taped over her forehead, and below it there was blood on her face. She was crying.

"Bernie," he said. "What happened. Are you all right?" He reached in for her, helped her out, pulled her to him in a crushing hug. "I've been scared to death," Chee said. "I've been terrified."

"Me too," Bernie said, her voice muffled against his shirt. "I'm still shaking."

"Oh, Bernie," Chee said. "I was afraid I'd lost you. What happened to you here? Why are you crying."

Bernie produced a sort of a choked-off laugh. "That will take a long time to explain," she said. "And you're about to crush me."

He relaxed the hug, but just a little. "Who did that to you?" Chee said, voice grim. "Someone hit you. We've got to get you to a doctor."

"How did you find me here?" Bernie said. "And why were you looking for me."

"Because I love you," Chee said. "Because I want to take you home where you'll be safe."

"Oh," Bernie said. She returned the hug, and then she was crying again.

Dashee's voice interrupted this. "Hey," he shouted. "We've got a dead man in here."

Dashee was standing in the open doorway of the shed, pointing in. "He's on his back on the floor. Looks like he fell off a chair." He leaned through the doorway, looking inside. "Blood on the floor, too. And a rifle. Looks like I may have myself my very first homicide as a Federal Bureau of Land Management Security Officer."

Bernie released her hold on Chee and slumped backward onto the car seat, shaking again.

"It's all right, Bernie," Chee said. "It's OK. Take it easy for a while."

Dashee was hurrying up. "Yeah, Bernie. And then tell us what happened."

"It was awful," Bernie said. "The man who was supposed to kill me, he didn't want to do it, and he had gotten my pistol from the Seamless Weld man somehow, and so Mr. Winsor was going to shoot him, and—" She was crying again.

"Stay here with Bernie," Chee said. "And call for some medical help. I'll go in and take a look."

What he saw was as Dashee had described it. A well-dressed, stocky, middle-aged man sprawled on his back beside an overturned chair. Chee squatted beside him. Shot in the chest, but the blood that had spread from under him obviously must have come from the exit wound. What he could see was already drying. He scanned the room quickly, noted the pipeline mechanism, noted the row of sacks filled with a white substance, noted the dirty yellow ball on one end, the screw cap beside it, and the white sacks still jammed inside.

Leaphorn had it right, Chee thought. **Naturally, Leaphorn had it right.** The contraption of pipes grown out of the floor was a trap for pipeline-cleaning pigs. And a pressure-release mechanism on its top was whistling—probably a signal another pig was arriving. The ball on the table must be a pig and its guts, now spilled, was probably cocaine. Enough to over-dose a thousand users. Quite a pig.

Chee rushed out into the sunlight. "Did you contact anyone? Are they sending an ambulance?"

"Bernie had already called the New Mexico State Police," Dashee said. "And she called her dispatcher. They said they'd sent a helicopter."

"Who hit you?" Chee asked. "Was it that man in there?"

"Where's his car?" Dashee asked. "What in the world happened?"

"Did you shoot him, Bernie? What happened to your pistol?"

"Stop! Stop! Stop!" Bernie shouted. "If you two will just shut up, stop asking questions, and be quiet, I'll try to tell you."

And she did. Starting with climbing on the car hood to look through the window and being surprised by three men.

"Three men!" A loud exclamation, jointly emerging from Chee and Dashee, both of whom were leaning against the car, looking down at her.

"Three," Bernie said. "The one in there. He's the one who hit me. His name is Winson, or Winsor, or Willson, or something like that. Winsor I think it was. He was the boss of the other two. He's the one who hit me and he's the one who said I had to be killed. One of the others—a big tall man, looked like an athlete, sort of red hair, sort of looked like an Irishman, but he spoke Spanish, and Winsor said his name was Budge C. de Baca, like that old Spanish family in New Mexico—anyway, he worked directly for Winsor, and from what Winsor said, he had assigned Budge the job of killing me."

"Killing you? Killing you?" Chee said.

Bernie ignored him. "The other one was wearing army fatigues and his name was Diego de Vargas and he spoke Spanish, too. And that bunch of pipes—"

"Bernie," Dashee said, "where are those two men? Are they armed? Do they have your pistol? Did they drive away? Where did they go?"

"They went away," Bernie said. "And I don't know where my pistol is. And do you want to hear this or not?"

"Sorry," Dashee said, and looked repentant.

So Bernie told them what happened in the shed, about the yellow round ball arriving, the sacks of cocaine taken out of it, and about the big man whispering to her that she should tell Winsor she was with the DEA and that she could be bribed. And all the rest of it, skipping back to report how de Vargas had taken her pistol but somehow Budge had gotten it.

"And then when Budge acted like he wasn't going to kill me, and was telling Winsor they couldn't get away with it, then Winsor told him to do it like, like . . ." Here Bernie's voice faltered. She paused a moment with her hands over her face. Then went on. "Like they had killed some woman named Chrissy, by throwing her out of an airplane into the ocean. Except they would throw me out over the mountains down in Mexico." She paused again, then hurried through it. "Then Winsor cocked his rifle and swung it around at Budge, and I was sitting there on the table right beside his chair, and I kicked at his arm and he hit me with the rifle."

Bernie stopped, looked at Chee and then at Dashee. Both seemed to be holding their breath, silent, waiting.

"Then, he shot, right beside my ear. Or maybe they both shot. And the next thing I knew I was lying on the table with one of those bags under my head, and Budge was using a handkerchief or something to stop the bleeding on my cheek and asking me how I felt, and it was then he said he didn't kill Chrissy." She stopped, looked at them, awaited the next question.

"Bernie," Chee said. "I want you to stop being a policeman. I want you to do something safe. I want you to marry me. I'll get rid of that trailer and we'll find a nice house and—"

And Dashee said, "Damn it, Chee, hold that for later. Let Bernie tell us where those two bastards went. They're getting away."

And Bernie said: "Oh, Jim, I don't want to be a policeman anymore."

And Dashee said: "But where did they go? They're driving off somewhere right now. Getting away."

"I don't know where they went," Bernie said. "While Budge was getting the blood off of my face he was talking to Diego de Vargas. Talking about flying. They would fly down to some place in Mexico. He had left this woman down there.

Chrissy. To keep her safe from Winsor. He said he was in love with this Chrissy, and would go down there and marry her, and then they would take her somewhere Budge had friends, and Vargas could sell the airplane and they would both start over. And, I don't know, I was trying to listen but I was feeling dizzy, and I was still scared, and they were talking mostly in Spanish. It was confusing."

"That airplane. Where is it?" Chee asked. "I guess this Budge must be the pilot for that man in the building, must be his personal pilot. There's probably some sort of airport at the ranch. At least a landing strip."

"Let's go find that airplane," Dashee said.

Chee was looking up. "I think we're a little late again."

The sleek white shape of the Dessault Falcon 10 appeared just over the ridge beyond the playa valley—trailing the sound little jet engines make when accelerating.

"Flying south," Dashee said. "In ten minutes he's over Mexico. Home free."

"I heard him telling this Diego de Vargas guy about Chrissy. She was a law clerk for Winsor, and Winsor told her he would marry her, and she got pregnant, and he ordered Budge to kill her so she wouldn't tell Winsor's wife."

"They're getting away," Dashee said, still staring toward the south where the Falcon had vanished.

"I hope so," Bernie said, sounding slightly woozy. "He really was in love with this Chrissy. He was telling that other man, the Mexican, about her. About how the boss told him to kill her but instead he took her down to Mexico and just told the boss she was dead. He was going there to get her."

"Hey!" Dashee said. "Going where?" He turned to Chee. "We can get him there. Where was he going?"

Bernie held her hand up to her forehead, touched the bandage over the bruise. "I don't remember," she said.

The diminishing whine of the jet's engines was replaced by the thunking sound of the Border Patrol's helicopter. It came in low, looking for the best landing spot. Only a moment later, that noise was joined by the siren of a State Police car bumping its way down the track toward the building site.

"They'll take you to the hospital at Las

Cruces, Bernie. It's the nearest one. I may have to stay here with Cowboy to try to explain all this. He reached into the car and hugged her to him, gingerly. Stay there. I'll come and get you."

"I don't think I'll be going anywhere for a while," Bernie said. "I'm the only witness."

26

Bernie was right. First to arrive was a New Mexico State Police sergeant with a patrolman. They were informed only with a secondhand, passed-along version of what Bernie had told her Border Patrol dispatcher. The sergeant wanted to know which one of them had done the shooting, where was the gun, who was the victim, was that stuff in the little packages some "controlled substance." Chee's efforts to add some clarity to this were interrupted by Dashee, who showed his credentials as a U.S. Bureau of Land Management enforcement officer. Dashee began an account of how the cocaine had arrived, which was interrupted by the arrival of a Guadalupe County Sheriff's car, occupied by a deputy and an undersheriff. This produced a flurry of discussion of who had jurisdiction here, which reminded Bernie that she, as a Customs patrol officer of the U.S. Treasury Department, was actually the officer in charge. But Bernie's head was still aching, and the bruise hurt. She wisely decided to stop resisting the orders of the paramedic who had arrived in the Border Control copter, to recline on the stretcher and take the pain pills he was pressing on her.

The undersheriff sent his deputy back to the Tuttle Ranch headquarters to confirm the plane was missing and to join the State Police patrol-man in making sure roadblocks were at work in case the two unaccounted-for males had driven away in the victim's missing Range Rover. About then, a dark blue Ford roared up and braked to a stop in a billowing cloud of dust.

Chee had been standing beside the copter, holding the hand of Bernie, who was looking very, very sleepy now. "Who's that?" Bernie asked.

"Blue Ford sedan," Chee said. "Two men getting out. Well dressed. Must be the FBI."

A few minutes later, the taller of the two came hurrying over. He flashed his FBI shield, said he was Special Agent something-or-other, checked Chee's identity, and looked at Bernie.

"Officer Manuelito? Right? You must have

heard those two men talking after the shooting. Did you hear where they were going?"

"She's in pretty bad shape," Chee said. "Possible concussion. You should wait until—"

"Stand aside," Special Agent said, motioning Chee away. "No time to wait. We want those men."

But Bernie had drifted off into morphine-induced dreams. Or perhaps she was pretending. And thus the paramedic and the copter pilot flew her away to the hospital at Las Cruces, and she missed the arrival of an SUV occupied by Drug Enforcement Agents, and the resulting dispute over which of the agencies had jurisdiction, which was eventually resolved by the arrival of someone representing Homeland Security, who declared himself in charge of the FBI, the DEA, the Border Patrol, the Department of Land Management, and the Navajo Tribal Police.

Sergeant Chee didn't argue. He was rushing Cowboy Dashee to the BLM vehicle to begin a high-speed journey to Las Cruces to make sure Bernie was being treated gently. And to take her home.

27

Some time passed before Chee could take Customs Patrol Officer Bernadette Manuelito anywhere. First there was an X ray, which showed no fractures, and then stitches to close the deep cut below her hairline, all of which led to two days of doctor-ordered bed rest in the hospital. There she was visited by an amiable FBI agent named Jenkins. He was black, middle-aged by Bernie's standards, and delighted her by bringing up the same questions that had been troubling her. Why had she been sent to that Tuttle Ranch gate site? What had her supervisor told her she was looking for? How about the "special arrangement" to cooperate with the ranch? And how had the photograph Henry had taken of her, wearing her Big

Thunder pin, gotten so quickly into the hands of Mexican drug dealers?

That, above all, stimulated Jenkins's interest, turned him away from nagging her about where she thought Budge and Diego might have gone, or what their real names might be. It sent him out the room to use his cell phone where she couldn't hear him. When he came back, he was in a hurry. Just asked Bernie if she had anything else to tell him, said: "Well, thank you then," and was gone.

The nurse came through the door after him.

"There's someone out in the hall waiting to see you. You ready for a visitor?"

Bernie was at the closet, getting her uniform on. "I'm ready to get out of here. Go home." She stopped buttoning her shirt, made a wry face. "Is it another policeman?"

"It's your young man."

It was the first time Bernie had heard anyone call Jim Chee "her man." But now, she thought, the nurse had it right. And it sounded fine.

"Give me a few minutes to get dressed and then send him in," Bernie said.

EPILOGUE

And so it was. The Sinister Pig was dead, the Pig Trap end of the Sinister Pipeline was safely in the hands of the federals, with the FBI, the DEA, and the Customs Service pushing and shoving for media credit and TV time. Now the TV crews are gone from the south gate of Tuttle Ranch, and the scimitar-horned oryx are grazing there again and all the other players are gone.

First to go were Budge and Diego de Vargas in the Falcon 10, which seemed to belong to the late Rawley Winsor but which, officials of his A.G.H. Industries would be surprised to know, was actually on the A.G.H. inventory. The Falcon is now in the hanger of another of A.G.H. subsidiaries, refueled and refurbished, waiting for Diego to fly it to Jamaica where its paint job and license numbers will be suitably revised.

Budge had flown south too, serving as copilot and instructor, using the Falcon's phone to call the Mazatlán hotel where Chrissy was installed, telling her what had happened and that he would be at her hotel in two hours.

When the Falcon pulled into the transient aircraft space, she was there waiting. A passionately romantic scene ensued. But who can tell what the future holds for such a pair.

Bureau of Land Management Security Officer Cowboy Dashee, having been the only officer left at the scene with even a hint of jurisdiction, was stuck at the south gate locale until sundown, answering the questions of various other federal officers and working on the explanation he would give his BLM boss for why he was involved in a drug bust more than two hundred miles south of where he was supposed to be.

Joe Leaphorn, the retired Legendary Lieutenant, who had been nowhere near the south gate, didn't escape the aftermath. Professor Louisa Bourbonette, back from her oral history roamings, handed him the telephone.

"Joe," she said, "it's someone named Mary Goddard, and she sounds angry."

She was. "Mr. Leaphorn, I remind you that when we exchanged information you promised me, a solemn promise, to tip me on any pertinent developments. I thought I could trust you."

"Well," said Joe, "ah—"

"Listen to this headline from my competitor's front page: 'Socialite Mogul Slain in Drug Raid.'"

"I know," Leaphorn said. "But I wasn't—"

"Wasn't what?"

"Down there," Leaphorn said. "Anyway, your story was the missing money from the tribal trust funds. All that royalty money that—"

"My story was why Stein was killed. The guy with the phony Carl Mankin credit card."

"I still don't know."

"Well, your people out there do," Goddard said. "Let me read it to you."

Leaphorn heard the sound of paper rustling.

"Here it is: 'Officer Manuelito said the conversations she overheard between Winsor and the two men working indicated Stein was killed because the drug dealers believed he was investigating their efforts to use pipeline cleaning devices to smuggle cocaine in from Mexico.'

"'She said Winsor had come to believe that Stein was actually working for a prominent senator—seeking evidence of pipeline use to illegally divert oil or gas shipments in the Interior Department scandal.'" Goddard stopped. "What do you say to that?"

"My only excuse is ignorance."

"Ignorance! I heard that you provided the tip that something funny was going on with that old pipeline."

"Not exactly," Leaphorn said.

"Well, no use yelling at you. What can you tell me now?"

"All I know is what I've been reading in the **Farmington Times,**" Leaphorn said. "Nobody cares about that Stein killing anymore. Maybe the next time we have a big story out here I can make it up to you."

"Big story out there? Fat chance."

Leaphorn should have said **almost** nobody cared about the Stein case. Sergeant Jim Chee still cared. He was now sitting at his desk staring at the computer screen in his crowded trailer home on the banks of the San Juan River. Stein had been murdered right in the territory he was responsible for. Even though the FBI had taken over and declared it a hunting accident he had to write a report on it. He was down to the concluding paragraph, and what could he say in conclusion?

He typed: "Evidence developed in a subsequent drug investigation strongly suggested"—someone was tapping at this screen door—"that Mexican interests in a drug-smuggling venture ordered Stein killed, believing he might reveal their plan."

It was Bernie, a neat bandage protecting the stitches on her face and the remains of her bruises still visible.

He ushered her in, noticed she was eyeing the interior of his trailer with an unusually intent interest. He hugged her.

"Bernie," he said, "you are absolutely beautiful, and if you'll marry me, I will never let anyone hit you with a rifle again."

Bernie returned the hug. "In that case, I'll marry you, providing you help me push this trailer down into the river so we can build a real house here."